MARCUS SAIEVA

To Be Frankie

A Christmas Story

outskirtspress
DENVER, COLORADO

To Be Frankie
A Christmas Story
All Rights Reserved.
Copyright © 2016 Marcus Saieva
v2.0 R1.1

Outskirts Press, Inc.
http://www.outskirtspress.com

ISBN: 978-1-4787-6834-0

Outskirts Press and the "OP" logo are trademarks belonging to Outskirts Press, Inc.

PRINTED IN THE UNITED STATES OF AMERICA

To my son Jedidiah, with love.

Merry Christmas!

A Pond -

" Is the earth's eye, looking into which the beholder measures the depth of his own nature."

- Henry David Thoreau

Chapter One

Dragonflies scattered in panic as the largemouth bass broke the pond's surface. A fishhook with a dangling worm pierced the bass's lip while the fish shook its head back and forth in defiance. With a loud splash the bass turned and took the worm down to the depths of the pond.

Seventeen-year-old Frankie Vincente's grip tightened on his fishing rod. His wavy dark brown hair flew back from his face and his hazel eyes widened.

"Got a big one!" he yelled.

He bent backward and his fishing rod bowed. "He's taking out line!"

His reel clicked with excitement, and the fight was on. I can do this, I've been fishing here all my life, Frankie thought.

"Whoa, whoa, whoa, why did my reel stop clicking?"

Quickly he cranked the reel, fighting the powerful fish. "No, no."

The reel clicked again, as the bass continued to take out line. The muscles in Frankie's forearms tensed. Then, nothing, no line was going out, no line was being reeled in. Puzzled and confused, he stared at the limp line floating in the water.

"I'm reeling you in again, Mr. Bass!" he said.

Frankie was dumbfounded as he watched his red and white bobber land on the bank followed by the empty hook drawing a thin line through the mud. He stood at the edge of the pond staring into the still water. "You got away!"

Some stuffing flew out of his old worn-out easy chair at the pond's edge when Frankie plopped down on it. He sat back, zipping up his jacket while taking in the peaceful surroundings as dusk set in. I feel safe at my pond. It's nice here.

Slumped in his chair under the oak tree, Frankie glanced across the water, inhaling deeply. It smells so fresh at the pond, he thought. He watched colorful dragonflies darting back and forth across the water. He turned his head toward a bullfrog croaking. On the other side of the pond were patches of pampas grass and tall reed-like cattail plants. The cattails won't bloom until spring, he thought.

Frankie reached down and grabbed his rod and tackle with a sigh of defeat. His fish hook and bobber dangled from the rod's thin tip. He stood up and turned in a full circle admiring his surroundings. Rows of dormant grape vines that made up his family's orchard flowed through the land.

Chapter Two

Something caught Frankie's attention; he noticed it moving on the ground. It was a glistening greenish-blue dragonfly stuck on its back in the muddy bank with its legs clawing at the air for mercy.

"Hey little dragonfly, I won't hurt you. There you go. Wow, you seem magical. I've never held a dragonfly. There you go, flip over in my hand. Ok, I'll hold you up as high as I can. Don't die, go on, fly away now," Frankie said.

The dragonfly wiggled a little, and then flew from Frankie's hands across the pond and returned to him, hovering at face level. He could have sworn her tiny eyes met his with gratitude. Frankie was amazed when she turned quickly and in a sparkling dash of iridescent greens, yellows, and blues, flew off like Tinkerbell across the sky.

"Goodbye Tinkerbell, fly on!" Frankie said.

His feet crunched the dried oak leaves as he walked away with his tackle box in one hand and his fishing rod bouncing in the other. I'll get that big bass one of these days. I don't think I did anything wrong. Sometimes my mind seems to work in reverse. Let's see what's for dinner.

Frankie examined the dry grapevines as he walked through the rows of the orchard. As if the vines could hear him, he said, "For now you're brown and dry, but don't worry, you'll have big green leaves and big purple grapes in the spring and summer time."

Frankie made it out of the grape vines and stepped onto the dirt road, heading for home.

The year was 1974. It was a cool Friday evening in December at Frankie's home in the San Joaquin Valley, California. His home was a two-story estate house with six bedrooms and maid's quarters. It was built in 1910 and restored to its original vintage style. An old black asphalt driveway lined with beautiful oak and pepper trees led to the home. Behind the home and down a dirt drive stood a small one-bedroom cottage next to the grape packing shed. The entire Vincente property was surrounded by the family's hundred-acre orchard.

Frankie's feet drummed up the oak steps of the stairway to his room. He set his fishing rod next to his other lonely rod in the corner of his bedroom. All of the sudden Frankie had a sad feeling overtake him and he wiped away a tear.

I wish I had a friend to fish with. And, why won't they let me play baseball? Why do they pick on me at school? Why do they beat me? If this bullying doesn't stop it will kill me. All I want to do is play baseball and have a friend to fish with.

Frankie's bedroom was large with twelve-foot-high ceilings. He had a regulation size basketball hoop and net high up on the wall. His floors of solid oak were covered with a big round rug. He had his own private bathroom. On the wall over his bed hung a San Francisco 49ers pennant and a poster of his favorite 49ers football player, John Brodie, the famous 1970s quarterback.

Frankie kept a clean room, other than an occasional ball or two left on the floor.

He picked up his orange sponge basketball and took a long shot across his room for the hoop and net. "Three point shot!"

The ball arched and then bounced off the orange rim. Slapping his hands together in defeat, he said, "Darn, missed again!"

Staring out his window at the back of his home, Frankie thought the farmland looked peaceful.

Chapter Three

Frankie's twenty-two-year-old sister Anna quietly stooped down in front of Frankie's closed door, listening in with her hand cupped to her ear. She heard water running. Good, he's in the shower, she thought.

Sliding her long slender fingers down the bannister, Anna moved gracefully but quickly down each oak step. Landing at the bottom of the stairs with a light jump, her straight shiny black hair flew before resting at the middle of her back. Anna's big green eyes and smile always lit up a room with a glow of cheer and beauty.

Anna sat on the sofa in her pajamas with her legs crossed Indian style. She was looking through a scrapbook on her lap when Nanny entered the room. She preferred to be called Nanny although her real name was Elaine.

"Oh, hello, Nanny," Anna said.

"Good evening, dear Anna."

"Why are you in full uniform, Nanny?"

"Anna dear, I am a sixty-year-old Nanny trained in the finest school in England. I will always maintain proper etiquette." While straightening her blonde hair that was up in a bun, Nanny's light blue eyes glanced down at Anna.

"I've been your and Frankie's Nanny from the day you were born, little girl. What is that you're looking at, Anna?" Nanny said.

Anna skimmed through the scrapbook, her green eyes dripping a tear.

"Please don't tell Frankie. I put this scrapbook together

a while back. It has his baseball photos, letters from baseball scouts from different colleges, and even a copy of his scholarship to UCLA," Anna said.

"Oh Anna, this is so special. You put together a memoir book of Frankie's accomplishments before his injury occurred. Before he ripped his leg open climbing that chain link fence out in left field that day. He had just turned 17. It has already been eleven months since it happened," Nanny said.

"Nanny, that was a very difficult time. Why did his leg have to get infected so badly? Why did he have to contract spinal meningitis? We almost lost him to that darn infectious disease, Nanny."

"Don't cry. We must be positive and strong for our dear lad. After all, he could have lost his leg, and his scar isn't that bad. It's only a few inches long."

"I know, I know, but the spinal meningitis damaged his brain. He was doing so well. He was so smart that he was in advanced classes and he was going to be graduating high school at seventeen years old, and he had a bright college career ahead of him. Now Frankie has the mentality of a 14-year-old boy. But, he's 17, Nanny. My brother is seventeen years old and he's back in the ninth grade!"

"Cheer up, Anna. I know it's tough on everyone seeing that the doctors put Frankie back in the ninth grade to match his mental capacity. But, they did say that in the future his mental state may catch back up to his actual age. Sometimes I can see the young man in him, but most times he does act like a boy," Nanny said.

"Look Nanny, here's a photo of Frankie's baseball team jumping all over him when he hit the home run to win his high school championships!" Anna said.

Nanny's British accent delighted Anna. "Cheers, bravo!"

Nanny said.

In the steamy bathroom, Frankie grabbed the shower fau-cet and turned the water off. The last drip of water trickled from the shower head. One, two, three, four, five, six, oh why do I count the tiles in the shower and other random things sometimes? Ah yes, that hot water felt great, he thought.

"Look at this photo, Nanny. Look how happy Frankie was when he was rounding home plate," Anna said.

Nanny looked so proper in the way she clapped her hands. "That's our boy!" she said.

Frankie was finishing getting dressed and poked his head out of his bedroom. "When is dinner ready?" he said.

Instantly Anna leaped from the sofa. "Nanny, hide the scrapbook in your room, quickly!" Anna said.

Frankie walked down the stairs towards Anna. "Hi Anna. Why are you rinsing your face in the kitchen sink?" he said.

"Uh, I got something in my eye," Anna said.

"Girls are silly," Frankie said.

After eating his dinner, Frankie rose from the table. "Please excuse me, Nanny, I'm going to my room now."

"Excuse yourself to your good sister as well, Frankie," Nanny said.

Jokingly, Frankie said, "Do I have to? All right, excuse me, Anna."

Anna tilted her head and with a grin, said, "You're ex-cused, brother."

"Oh, Nanny, your homemade vegetable soup and biscuits were yummy, yummy, yummy," he said and headed back up to his room, rubbing his full stomach. He shut the door be-hind him and sat at his desk in thought. I guess I'll work on my math homework. Why is math so hard for me? I won't give up until I figure this out.

Chapter Four

Lying on his back under the covers, Frankie blinked a couple of times as he awoke. The morning sun beaming through the window warmed his face. He stood up yawning and stretching his arms over his head in his favorite San Francisco 49ers pajamas.

When he saw his football on the floor he bent down and picked it up and raised it over his shoulder as if playing in a game.

"I'm the 49ers quarterback. I'm John Brodie! Tied score, three minutes left in the game. We need a touchdown! No one opened to the left, no one open to the right," he said. "Finally a man opened in the end zone!"

Frankie released the ball full force aiming for the green cushiony chair in the corner of his room. But he missed. The ball made a loud bam, hitting the wall inches from the window.

Frankie stood with his hands covering his mouth. Oh shoot! He said.

Anna flung Frankie's door open. "What was that, are you okay, Frankie? My gosh it sounded like Papa's gun going off!" she said.

"It's okay Anna. Do you really think I would misuse papa's gun? I just missed the chair with my football and it hit the wall, that's all."

Anna heard Nanny running up the wooden steps. "It's okay, Nanny, it was just a football," Anna said.

Nanny grasped the wooden handrail catching her breath

for a moment before heading back downstairs.

A sweet aroma led Frankie down the stairs. Yumm, I can smell blueberry pancakes and bacon cooking.

A slice of butter melted down the sides of Frankie's pancakes followed by trickles of maple syrup touching the bacon. Aroma filled the room. Frankie savored every bite of blueberry pancake, followed by the crunchiness of the farm fresh bacon.

"Thank you for breakfast, Nanny," Frankie said.

When Frankie opened the tall oak front door wide enough to carry his fishing rod and tackle box through, the blueberry and bacon aroma seemed to follow him outside. Closing the heavy door behind him, Frankie turned and walked down the red brick steps into the day. The sights, smells, and sounds of the kitchen changed to blue skies, fresh country air, trees and birds singing.

Frankie enjoyed seeing the pond on that beautiful day. He poked the hook through the slimy worm and a small trickle of blood ran down his finger.

"Sorry, Mr. Wiggler," he said.

Frankie watched his line fly out with the squirming worm soaring over the water.

He sang his fishing-wish. "Gonna catch a trout, I have no doubt, or maybe it's a bass I pull out a class, catfish, catfish put you on my dish!" he sang.

The worm plopped in the water. "I got a hit!" Frankie said.

Immediately he started reeling something in. He reeled and reeled, then flung the fish on the pond's bank.

"It's a sunfish," he said.

"Got to hurry and get the hook out of you, Mr. Sunfish. Hold still let me take the hook out of your lip without hurting you. Whoa, you're a slimy little fellow. There you go, swim away now," Frankie said.

With finesse Frankie maneuvered a fresh worm onto the fish hook, cast out and stood ready.

"I got one! Wahoo! The sunfish are biting," He said.

As Frankie reeled in another fish, no worries were on his mind. After he landed the third sunfish on the edge of the pond's bank, he released it in the water, and then rested in his chair.

Dragonflies danced in the air around the pond. An occasional butterfly fluttered by. Birds chirped. The warmth of the California sun caressed Frankie's face on the cool December morning.

Frankie's head started to gently bob up and down as he fell asleep in his old worn-out chair at the pond's edge.

When he fell asleep, Frankie didn't notice a big black raven sitting in the tall oak tree above him. The raven had yellow beady eyes like the color of courage. It cawed quietly once as to not wake the sleeping boy.

A toad croaked as if it were answering the raven. The raven looked down at Frankie, then all around. It was as if the raven were looking out for Frankie.

Frankie awoke in his chair. The pond is peaceful and fresh smelling, he thought. Suddenly, he heard kids playing baseball in the distance. Why won't they let me play? Why won't they let me play baseball with them?

Why won't they? He kept thinking while staring at the ground on his way home.

Frankie set his fishing rod in the corner next to his spare rod, in his bedroom. Will I ever have a friend to fish with? He thought. He sat on the edge of his bed, staring at the floor. Quietly Frankie's head sank into his pillow and he let out a sigh as his eyes closed.

Chapter Five

Oh dear, it's seven a.m. I don't hear Frankie yet. I'd better go make sure he's awake. I don't want him to miss the school bus, Nanny thought. Standing outside Frankie's bedroom door, she listened in. Her head tilted, Nanny held her knuckles in midair momentarily listening before knocking on the dark oak door.

"It's Monday morning, dear Lad. It's time for school. You must hurry for the bus," Nanny said.

Frankie's messy hair bounced as he jumped out of bed. Running for the bathroom he turned his head, noticing the time.

"I'm up, getting ready for school!" he said.

Frankie got dressed and scooted out the door, hurrying up the dirt road to the giant oak tree that marked his bus stop. I'm just a little late, but I should make it to the school bus. Mama and Papa told me I can never be late for school.

He hurried onto the yellow school bus right before the doors closed. Oh good, everyone is on the bus already. They can't do anything to me this morning. The sound of air brakes releasing pressure sounded off. Dust flew from the dirt road as the bus pulled away. Walnut Street School was a small country school that Frankie attended. The school went from kindergarten to ninth grade and had 270 students.

"Hand your math papers up towards the front of the class please," Mr. Conte said.

I hope I did okay on this math paper, Frankie thought.

Mr. Conte was the teacher for the eighth and ninth grade

class. Since there were only about a dozen kids in each class, the eighth and ninth graders were all in one room together. Sometimes they had the same assignments, and sometimes Mr. Conte split the assignments up for each grade. Mr. Conte's salt and pepper hair, and black rimmed glasses gave him an intelligent look. He taught in a way that the kids respected. Mr. Conte was a good teacher.

"Okay kids, you're excused for the day. Have a great evening," Mr. Conte said.

The sound of papers rustling and chairs scooting amongst the chatter filled the room.

When the school bus arrived back at the oak tree Frankie felt relieved. Everyone at the front of the bus is teasing about someone kissing. I think I can sneak off the bus while they are all teasing each other about whoever got kissed. Oh, this is good, really good, Frankie thought.

He put his head down and walked from the back of the bus to the front doors.

I did it. I got off easy this time. I better hurry. Monday's are always bad. They don't like that I get picked up from school by Anna on Fridays. Her red convertible Mustang is so hip. Should I run? No, I'll just speed walk out of here for home.

Frankie headed for home where Nanny was busy as always when she heard the phone ring. She picked it up. "Hello, Vincente residence, this is Nanny speaking."

"Hello, Elaine!" Maria said.

Maria was Frankie's mama. Maria was a good mother who loved her family. She was a pretty woman, half Italian and half Belgian. Her Belgian side came out in her sweet personality.

"Elaine, we are having a successful trip but it will be so nice to get home," Maria said.

Nanny stood tall and firm, as she didn't like when Maria didn't call her Nanny.

"Madam, you are my boss and you are not supposed to call me by my first name. I was trained at the famous school of etiquette in Cambridge London. And you are to address me as Nanny," Nanny said.

"Elaine, Elaine, you're the best Nanny in the world. But, you're like family. You've been with us for so long. I refuse to call you anything other than my dear Elaine," Maria said. "Anyway, dear Elaine, please tell Anna to pick us up at the small airport tomorrow at five p.m. And please make sure Frankie is there with her."

"Yes, Madam, I will tell her promptly."

"Thank you, and I'll see you tomorrow, Elaine," Maria said.

"Oh, hello Frankie, I didn't hear you come in. Dear lad, your mama and papa are arriving tomorrow at five p.m. You and Anna will pick them up at the small airport," Nanny said.

"Oh, good, mama and papa are coming home! I have to tell papa about the fish I caught," Frankie said.

Antonio Vincente, Frankie's father, was a humble hard-working man. He was a second generation Italian American. He came up the hard way with no money. Antonio slept in barns working for other farmers, but he saved his money for years until he bought his own grape orchard and raised a family. He was the owner of the famous Vincente grape juices and jams that he produced.

Chapter Six

"Come on, Frankie, let's go get Mama and Papa!" Anna said.

"I'm Coming, Anna!" Frankie said, putting on his brown skateboard shoes.

As they drove, Frankie said, "Wow, Anna, I can feel Papa's Suburban move when the wind hits us."

Anna gripped the big Suburban's steering wheel with both hands navigating with confidence. "You know it's windy when you can feel this big old truck bucking," Anna said.

Frankie lowered his visor. "The sun is right in my eyes."

Arriving at the little airport, Frankie held the glass entrance door open. "After you Anna."

Anna gracefully walked into the airport while straightening her hair. "Thank you Frankie."

"Why is the airport empty?" Frankie said.

"I don't know. Usually there are at least a couple people working," Anna said.

I guess this is how tiny airports are sometimes, Frankie thought. "Come over here, Anna. I want to watch mama and papa's plane land from this big window. Wow! Look at the orange wind sock. It's blowing hard. Papa taught me how the pilots use it to gauge the wind. When do they land?"

"Any minute now," Anna said.

"Here they come! I see their landing lights flashing in the sky. Papa taught me about them. See the lights, Anna!?"

"Oh, now I see them. I hope they can land in this wind," Anna said.

"The plane is swerving all over the place!" Frankie said.

"Oh my gosh, please make a safe landing, Mama and Papa," Anna said.

"Here they come," Frankie said. "The plane is blowing from side to side! Lower, lower, touchdown! Yippee, they made it home!"

The small plane rolled down the runway bucking in the wind. Frankie and Anna's cheering voices echoed through the empty airport.

Antonio could have kissed the ground, he was so happy to be back in the USA. Europe was nice but I love getting home, Antonio thought.

Once the family got loaded in the Suburban, they headed for home.

"You're doing a fine job driving this evening, Anna," Antonio said.

"What? You mean to say that I don't always drive well, Papa?"

"No, no, I didn't mean that, sweetheart. I'm just tired."

"You must both be exhausted. You flew home all the way from England," Anna said.

"I'm so happy to be home," Maria said.

"Yes, me too, honey. The San Francisco airport was crowded. Then we caught the small plane from there and the wind kicked up," Antonio said.

"I saw the wind sock blowing hard, Papa. Then I saw your plane coming in. You were blowing from side to side and up and down," Frankie said.

"Yes, son, it was a scary ride for your mama. But, I comforted her," Antonio said. Hearing his mama giggling, Frankie said, "What's so funny mama?"

"Kids, your brave papa was so scared, I felt his hand

sweating right through my Calvin Klein's," Maria said.

Laughter broke out in the Suburban as the Vincente's drove up their driveway through the oaks and pepper trees.

Chapter Seven

Frankie's alarm clock woke him with a sudden buzzing sound. He yawned and stretched in his bed. "Time for school," he said.

Frankie shut the front door behind him and proceeded to take on the day. As peaceful as the countryside was, Frankie's jaunts to school entailed daily fear. Burr, its cold this morning, he thought.

The huge oak tree that marked his bus stop grew closer as Frankie's footprints stamped into the dirt road. Oh good, it looks like Katie is the only one at the tree this morning.

Katie, who some people called Red-headed Kate, was a 14-year-old eighth grader. She was a good student.

"Good morning, Katie," Frankie said.

When Frankie approached Katie she whispered, "Frankie, listen up. Calvin's hiding behind the bushes with Chad and Billy. They're going to get you. Calvin said he'd slap me around and cut all my hair off if I told you."

Frankie's expression turned to an instant look of being on guard, like prey aware of a predator.

Calvin was a tall and thin fifteen-year-old ninth grader. He had an eerie, evil way about him. His followers, Chad and Billy, were also fifteen and in the ninth grade.

Katie's eyes widened with fear and she gasped when she saw Calvin spring from the bushes like an evil lion leaping onto its prey.

He kept shoving Frankie backward until they were hidden behind the bushes.

"Leave me alone!" Frankie said.

"You know what to do, Billy," Calvin said.

Billy's stuttering problem got worse whenever he was nervous. "Y-yes, I'm s-s-supposed to st-st-stall the b-bus," he said.

Billy ran to the dirt road, looking back and forth over his shoulder.

Calvin glared at Frankie. "I saw the smile on your face. What are you so happy about, rich boy? Did you enjoy getting a ride home from school in your sister's Mustang Friday? Huh, well did you? Does that make you happy, rich boy? Well, does it?"

"Get behind him now, Chad!" Calvin said.

Frankie was so terrified of Calvin that he didn't realize Chad was behind him on all fours.

Calvin grunted while tearing his knuckles into Frankie's stomach with a powerful punch. Just as quickly as Frankie buckled over, Calvin pushed him over the top of Chad.

"Thump," went Frankie's body in the dirt.

Billy's body straightened with tension when he saw the yellow school bus coming up the road. "Here c-c-comes the b-bus!" he said.

Frankie was down in the dirt holding his aching stomach begging the bullies to stop. "Please leave me alone, please, please have mercy," he said.

Calvin stooped over Frankie, glaring at him like a mad dragon ready to project fire. "You're never playing baseball! And, you damn sure will never play in the Christmas tournament! I run the team! I'm the star pitcher! Do you hear me, rich boy?" Calvin said.

Frankie lay in the dirt holding his stomach in pain. He

looked up at Calvin. "I've never done anything to you, I'm nice to everyone. If you don't stop bullying me it's going to kill me. Why do you do this to me?" he said.

Chad saw the bus idling under the oak tree with its two front doors opened.

"Calvin, the bus is waiting!" Chad said.

"Take this, rich boy!" Calvin said.

Calvin clenched his teeth and ran toward the idling bus, kicking up a cloud of dust, dirt, and pebbles into Frankie's face. "Just sit in the bus, Chad. I'll handle Mrs. Harrington," he said.

Mrs. Harrington was the thirty-year-old blonde bus driver. She loved her job and all the kids liked her.

Frankie pressed one hand in the dirt and the other hand on a knee and got up. His face stung like he had been attacked by wasps. He ran to the bus bent over, holding his stomach. "Wait for me, please, wait for me! Wait for me, Mrs. Harrington!" he called out to her.

Mrs. Harrington couldn't see Frankie running behind the bus. Dust rising from the big tires blocked her visibility. Coughing from the dust cloud, Frankie dropped to one knee in the middle of the dirt road, holding his stomach with one hand and reaching out with the other as if he were grabbing for the bus.

The yellow bus disappeared in the distance and the dust cleared, leaving behind a vast emptiness in his spirit. A tear made its way down through the dirt on his stinging cheek. He stood in pain on the road for a minute gathering himself as much as he could and then he headed for home.

"Why, why do they do this to me? What is it I have ever done?" Frankie said. His feet connected with care on each brick step and across the wooden porch. He opened the front door and poked his face in. No one in the living room or dining room. Trying not to cough while holding his stomach, he scooted up the stairway into his room and closed the door.

Chapter Eight

After sleeping it off for a while, Frankie washed his face in his bathroom sink. He watched dirty water trickle down the sink, wishing his bullied memories would follow into the depths of the drain. Drying his face he looked in the mirror attempting to forget the agony the bullies had caused to his spirit.

Okay, they're putting up Christmas decorations. I hear Mama, Anna, and Nanny downstairs. Papa is probably in his study or out in the orchard somewhere. It's a little after three o'clock. Time to head downstairs. I don't want anyone to know I get bullied, Frankie thought.

From upstairs Frankie saw Anna and Nanny carrying a big box of Christmas tree ornaments across the living room like two Santa's helpers. Perfect timing to head down, he thought.

"Oh, hi, Frankie. I didn't see you come in," Anna said.

"Hi, sis." Frankie noticed that Nanny seemed winded.

"Frankie, dear lad, help me on this end of the box," Nanny said.

While he helped Nanny with the box of ornaments, he admired the fifteen-foot-tall Christmas tree. It was like a tree you would see at the mall but real and with a strong scent of pine.

"Wow, nice Christmas tree! It smells good too," Frankie said.

"It was delivered while you were in school. You're just in time to join us in decorating it," Anna said.

"Where's Mama and Papa?"

"Papa's in the orchard and Mama's in the flower garden," Anna said.

Maria, graced with a smile, walked in the back kitchen door with her gardening hat and gloves. She was carrying a straw basket with clippings of red poinsettia Christmas flowers.

"Oh, there's my wonderful son!" Maria said. "Elaine, turn on some Christmas music please, dear."

Nanny said, "Madam, please call me Nanny. I have been trained…"

Anna broke in, "Uh, oh, here we go again. When will they get over this and just call each other what each other wants?"

Nanny cleared her throat and raised her chin to the side as if to not be interrupted.

"I have been trained at the finest school of etiquette in Cambridge, London. And, I am to refer to you as Madam and you are to refer to me as Nanny. I will never budge," Nanny said.

Shaking her head in disagreement, Maria would not give in. "Elaine, you have been with us for years, and you're family now. Just call me Maria. You don't have to call me Madam," Maria said.

Nanny stretched to the highest tree branch she could reach on the tree and hung the shiny red and green ornament.

Frankie watched the ornament dangling and it reminded him of the bobber on the narrow end of his fishing rod. He got a kick out of listening to his mama and Nanny's ongoing debate. To him it was like a ball game in overtime that would never end.

"I will never disregard proper etiquette, Madam," Nanny said.

Antonio had heard the two ladies debating as he walked

into the room. He leaned over and put his hand on Frankie's shoulder, looking in his eyes. "They've been at this debate for years, son, I don't think they will ever stop. I think it stimulates their blood," he said.

Frankie smiled and hugged Antonio. "Hi Papa!"

Frankie started to look through one of the boxes of ornaments and was happy to find his favorite. He hung his glass ornament of a fishing Santa who had a trout swinging from his little fishing rod. The ornament reminded Frankie of the pond.

Suddenly Frankie heard a rumble outside. "Papa, I hear trucks pulling up the driveway," he said.

Antonio glanced at his watch as if expecting something to occur.

"Oh good. It's the Christmas decorators for the outside," Antonio said.

Frankie looked out the window at the trucks pulling in. Oh, this means our Christmas Eve party is almost here. I love the party. Everyone is nice to me, Frankie thought. He'd almost forgotten about the beating he had taken at the bus stop, but the pain returned as he climbed the stairs. "I'm going to do my homework now," he said.

Chapter Nine

Frankie sat in class the following morning trying his best to concentrate on his school work.

"Class, after this film on the 'Necessity of the Sun' we will have physical education. I have a special treat for you today. Today we will play coed baseball for PE class," Mr. Conte said.

The class applauded and high fived each other with smiling faces at Mr. Conte's announcement.

Frankie lit up with mixed emotions of disbelief and excitement. "Did he say baseball? Wahoo!" he said.

Mr. Conte paced across the floor at the front of the class. "After baseball you will all take a test on the film. The test score will count towards your final grade."

Frankie in disbelief raised his hand. "Mr. Conte?"

"Yes, Frankie what is it?"

"Uh, can I play baseball, too?"

"Well, of course, Frankie. Why wouldn't you?" Mr. Conte said.

Calvin turned in his seat and glared at Frankie in the back row.

"Oh... just wondering, that's all. Thank you, Mr. Conte," Frankie said.

Katie, in a daring gesture, stuck her tongue out at Calvin, then turned to Frankie. "This is great, Frankie. You get to play ball!" Katie said.

Frankie had a great time playing baseball with his class under the supervision of Mr. Conte. After the game everyone returned to class, pulled out their chairs, and took a seat.

"Okay, class. Good ball game, now settle down in your seats and prepare for your test. Oh, and Frankie, nice home run," Mr. Conte said.

Katie tapped Frankie on the back of the shoulder from her seat behind him.

"Frankie, you were my star today. Your homerun was so cool," she said.

"Thank you, Katie. I had the best time in a long time," he said.

"I can help you with your math work tomorrow at lunch time if you want," Katie said.

"Okay. Thank you, Katie!"

"Pass your papers towards the front of the class. Class dismissed!" Mr. Conte said.

When Frankie walked outside the classroom, Calvin and his gang were waiting for him.

"The home run you hit off me was nothing but luck. Do you hear me, rich boy?" Calvin said. "Who do you think you are? You just got lucky. I run the school-team and you're never playing after school with us! You're never going to play in the Christmas morning tournament at the fairgrounds! You lame brain!"

The slap came out of nowhere and connected squarely on Frankie's cheek bone with a smacking sound.

"Ouch! Why did you slap me?" Frankie said.

Calvin grabbed Frankie's school books out of his hands, sending books and papers flying through the air.

Katie had been talking to the teacher before closing the door behind her. "Bye, Mr. Conte," she said. When she turned to walk down the corridor she saw Frankie in distress.

"Frankie, what happened? Here, let me help you," she said.

"Calvin got me again. Calvin said I will never play baseball with the team."

Katie helped Frankie pick up his papers and books with her head shaking and her blood boiling. "He's a jackass!" she said. "Come on, Frankie, let's get on the bus. Follow right behind me and we'll sit in the back."

Mrs. Harrington sat in the driver's seat looking at the oncoming kids through the double doors. "All aboard!" she said.

Frankie walked by Calvin with his head down, following Katie.

Katie gave Calvin a vicious glance as she walked by, saying, "You're just jealous of Frankie."

Katie sat down at the back of the bus with Frankie, shaking her head. "Don't have a long face, Frankie. You hit a nice home run. You're a hero today," she said.

The school bus approached the big oak tree. When Mrs. Harrington's foot pressed on the brakes, air shot out from under the bus. "All out for the oak tree stop!" she said.

Katie headed one way on the dirt road and Frankie headed the other way towards home.

Frankie stopped and turned back toward Katie with a curious look on his face and his palms turned up. "Katie, what's jealous mean?"

"I'll explain tomorrow at school. I've got to run," Katie said.

Before getting too far away Katie turned back around and watched Frankie heading home. "Have a good evening, Frankie!" she said.

But, Frankie didn't hear her. As he approached the red brick steps to his front porch, he began to cheer up.

Maria and Nanny were inside working on Christmas decorations.

"Mama, I'm a hero. Katie said I'm a hero because I hit a home run today at school."

Maria ran up and gave Frankie a big hug backed by a warm smile. "You're a hero with a home run? Well, look at you," she said.

Nanny lit up with joy and began singing to Frankie, "You're a jolly good fellow, you're a jolly good fellow."

Maria joined in. "Come on, Anna, dance and sing with us. All together now, and hold each other's shoulders. That's it, single file! Your brother is a hero, he hit a home run!" Maria said.

"You're a jolly good fellow, for you're a jolly good fellow, for you're a jolly good fellooow, that nobody can deny, nobody can deny!" They all sang and danced.

Antonio wiped the sweat from his forehead after coming in from the grape orchard. "What's this singing I hear?" he said.

"Come on, Papa, join in!" Frankie said.

Antonio laughed while observing his family for a moment before joining in the dance circle. "You're a jolly good fellow, you're a jolly good fellow," he sang. "Thank you everyone! It's nice to be appreciated," he said.

"Not you, Papa, me, I'm the jolly good fellow. I hit a home run today. I'm a hero, Katie told me."

"Oh, excuse me son, *you're* the jolly good fellow, which nobody can deny," Antonio sang.

The family danced around the house singing in a single file holding each other's shoulders. Nanny was the first to give in. She collapsed on the sofa laughing. "I can't take it any longer," she said.

One by one the Vincente's wore themselves out from all the fun.

"Frankie's the last one standing!" Antonio said.

Everyone cheered while Frankie danced and sang, until he finally dropped to his back on the rug, laughing.

"When is dinner ready, Nanny?" he asked.

"Well, dear lad, I was just going to announce that dinner is ready now," Nanny said.

"Thank you, Nanny. Time to wash up everyone," Frankie said.

"Yes Sir, Mr. Hero," Anna said.

Nanny was in classic form. "This evening you're having my English mincemeat pie and a side of potato dumplings topped with cranberry sauce. A meal fit for a hero," she said.

"Thank you, Nanny. It's one of my favorites," Frankie said.

"I love this dish, Elaine," Maria said.

Nanny started to correct Maria, saying, "Madam, I was trained in the finest..." then suddenly ran to the kitchen. "Oh gosh, I almost overcooked the cranberry sauce!" she said.

"Saved by the bell," Anna said.

When the family and Nanny were seated for dinner, Antonio took over. "Let's bow our heads in prayer. Dear Lord, thank you for your grace and thank you for this food we share together as a family. In the name of God, amen."

"Amen," everyone said.

Chapter Ten

Frankie watched the rain through his window while drifting off to sleep. Waking in the middle of the night, he recalled a dream: There was a small pig chasing me playfully through the grape vines. While I ran I looked over my shoulder at the little pig and I noticed the vines were bursting with huge purple grapes popping out from under big green leaves.

Then he fell asleep again, balanced on one elbow before sinking into the mattress with a snore. It rained through the night bringing a refreshing cleansing to the farmland. In the morning the sun shined through Frankie's wet window, casting colorful prism-like designs on his bed. He stared out his window at the dewdrops that hung from the eves. The rain had rinsed the dusty tractor and water dripped into a rusty pale. The green leaves on the trees seemed to be polished clean.

It cleared up this morning, Frankie thought.

After eating breakfast, Frankie stood at the front door ready to take on the wet day.

"Bye honey. Have a great day at school," Maria said.

"Bye Mama," Frankie said.

Frankie made his way up the road. The dirt road was sopping wet and looked like the frosting on a chocolate brownie.

"The air feels refreshing," Frankie said.

He heard a raven cawing in the huge oak tree at the bus stop. Frankie looked around the countryside as he walked. A red-headed woodpecker flew by. A blue jay perched on a wooden post at a barbed wire fence. Sparrows chirped in the trees. A big orange monarch butterfly flew by.

Frankie's eyes examined the area as he stood under the tree.

No one's here. Maybe everyone played hooky because of the rain. I'm glad I wore these old cowboy boots. They're already muddy. What do you keep cawing at, you old raven?

And, then it happened. Calvin yelled from behind the bushes. "Fire one!" he said.

"Roger that, Captain!" Chad said.

Calvin, Chad, and Billy started pummeling Frankie with moist dirt clods. Frankie tried his best to cover his face and head while under fire.

"Ouch! Stop it! Please stop!" Frankie said.

"Don't stop throwing until he cries bloody murder!" Calvin said.

"Please stop, ouch! Ouch my head! Please!" Frankie said.

Katie arrived and tried to cover Frankie while she took hits of her own. "Stop it, you lousy bullies, don't you understand he has brain damage?" she said.

"Hit her if she gets in the way!" Calvin said.

Frankie took hit after hit. Katie took some hits.

"Ouch!" Frankie said.

"Ouch, quit already, you jackasses!" Katie said. Then she pointed down the road. "The bus, the bus is coming!"

The three bullies ran behind the bushes and down to the creek.

"Run, dudes! Follow me!" Calvin said.

Frankie took a moment to catch his breath. "Thank you, Katie," he said.

"Here, Frankie let me help you brush off this dirt. Nope, it's too damp. I'm just smearing it all over your jacket. We'll clean up at school," she said.

Frankie held his head with both hands. "Ah, my head," he said. "Hey, Katie you were hit a couple times too."

"I'm okay, Frankie, here's the bus," she said.

"Good morning, kids. What's all this dirt on you two?" Mrs. Harrington said.

Katie nudged Frankie from behind as if to tell him to keep walking to the back of the bus. "Uh, we had a little friendly dirt clod fight, that's all, Mrs. Harrington."

"You're rubbing your head, Frankie. Are you okay?" Katie said.

"Yes, I'll be fine Katie, thank you."

Katie gave Frankie a caring hug when they got to school. "Go ahead into the boy's bathroom and clean up with damp paper towels. I'll do the same," she said.

"Okay, thank you," Frankie said.

Leaning over the white porcelain sink with the water running, Frankie broke down in tears.

Chapter Eleven

Frankie was much better once he realized the bullies weren't in class.

After class Frankie and Katie walked to the bus. "Class was nicer without the bullies here today," he said.

"Yes, there was a peaceful energy in the room today. Come on, Frankie, let's get on the bus."

"Katie, can you do me a big favor and tell Mrs. Harrington I'm going to walk home today?" Frankie said.

"You're going to walk home? Sure I can tell her for you. I would join you, Frankie, but I have to hurry home today."

"Okay, maybe we can walk another day, Katie. I'll walk alone and enjoy the sunshine now that it's out and I might even stop by the pond on the way home."

"Okay, have a nice walk, Frankie. I'll see you tomorrow. And, I'll tell Mrs. Harrington for you."

"Okay. Bye, Katie," Frankie said.

Frankie turned the corner and began his jaunt home. He headed up the dirt road absorbing the moment. The sun shined through the cotton-ball sky, birds sang and danced about the freshly rinsed terrain. Trees and wooden fence posts retained rainy moisture like a rain forest. Frankie passed by an olive orchard, then an orange grove. Up ahead were a pig farm on the left and a goat farm on the right. He looked over his shoulder and saw the school bus coming.

In a burst of energy Frankie yelled out, "I'm going to try to beat the bus home!"

As Frankie sprang in to a full sprint, a big black raven flew overhead as if it were guiding him down the road. The race was on. Frankie was running as fast as he could while the yellow bus gained on him.

Mrs. Harrington leaned forward in her seat. "Katie, it looks as if Frankie is racing us to the tree!" she said.

Katie ran up to the front seat where Calvin usually sat, leaped onto the cushiony vinyl, pushed down the little window, and peered out. "He's doing pretty well!" she said.

"Prepare to pass our running opponent!" Mrs. Harrington said.

Frankie gave it all he had, his arms pumping back and forth to the beat of his fast moving feet.

Katie yelled out her window to Frankie, "Go Frankie, go!" she said.

All the school kids were looking out the right side of the bus at Frankie, cheering him on. Mrs. Harrington caught up to him and stayed with him side by side for a moment. She looked at Frankie with a large glowing smile and excited eyes. Frankie's eyes locked with hers, returning the same look of excitement.

Frankie ran faster with all he had. Then Mrs. Harrington tilted her head back in laughter while shifting gears. Frankie's pace slowed to a jog as the yellow school bus sped away.

Children laughed and waved to Frankie out the back windows. He stopped on the side of the dirt road, bent over laughing and drawing in air at the same time. When he looked up at the bus flying down the dirt road he saw a reddish glow behind a hand giving a thumbs up.

That's Katie's red hair, that's her giving me a thumbs up, Frankie thought.

The raven was cawing like mad from its perch on a fence post catching Frankie's attention. Something didn't sound right. Frankie straightened up catching his breath and listening. He heard a blood curdling scream. It sounds like it's coming from Farmer Bob's pig farm, Frankie thought.

The strange sound turned to a frightening screaming gurgle. And then Frankie saw it. "Oh my gosh! A little pig has his head stuck in the fence!" Frankie said. Adrenaline took over in Frankie's brain and he flew to the dying pig.

"Don't die, don't die!" he said. Without even realizing what he was doing, Frankie ran across the pig sty into a shed.

"Farmer Bob, Farmer Bob, help! Where are you? Help, Farmer Bob, help!" Frankie said.

Farmer Bob never showed up. Frankie ran to a work bench and began rifling through old rusty tools. "Yes, wire cutters," he said.

As he ran out of the shed, his foot slipped in the mud and he went down in the pig sty with the rusty wire cutters falling into the mud in front of his face.

The young pig's cry for mercy became a desperate wheeze. It drew in just enough air to keep itself alive. Frankie tried to slide the wire cutters between the wire and the pig's neck, but they wouldn't fit.

"Darn it, don't die!" Frankie said.

Frankie's heart pounded in his chest like a bass drum. He had no other choice than to press so hard that it cut the pig's neck. When the clippers cut the first wire the little pig's wheeze deepened. When the clippers cut through the second wire the pig's head popped out of the fence squirting blood. Frankie fell back in the mud with the pig in his arms.

"Breathe, breathe!" he said.

The pig's wheezing deepened with each attempt to fill its lungs with air. Then with one big cough it spit something up that looked like reddish-brownish slime, before taking a deep long desperate breath of air.

"That's it, little pig, breathe, again, breathe," Frankie said.

Frankie had no idea how much time passed before the color returned to the pig's face and it nodded off to sleep. The trauma had exhausted both Frankie and the pig.

Frankie didn't know where he was when he awoke under the stars, sitting against a fence post in a pig sty, holding a pig in his arms with dried blood on its neck. Then it came back to him when the thankful pig looked in Frankie's eyes and started oinking as Frankie hugged it.

"You made it, little pig, you lived," he said. "Oh no, everyone is going to be worried about me. I have to get home immediately!"

After setting the pig down safely in its sty Frankie darted off for home. When he got close to home he felt something nudge his lower leg and he jumped.

"Hey little pig, what in the heck are you doing? You have to stay in your pig sty. Oh my gosh, I'll have to run you back," he said.

When Frankie set the pig back in its sty the little pig went berserk with wailing oinks.

Frankie glared and pointed his finger at the defiant little pig. "I already saved your life. Now what do you want! You're going to get me into all kinds of trouble. Stay here, I tell you, stay here!"

Again Frankie darted off for home, walking fast in the night. When the pig let out a deep bellowing oink right behind him, Frankie jumped and let out a scream. When he saw the little pig, he couldn't help laughing. When he spoke to the pig it got all happy and excited.

"You scared me little pig, its dark out here. I didn't see you coming. You want to be my pig, don't you? Okay, okay, come on home with me. I'll clean you up and put you in the garden shed for tonight. Uh, I'll just name you "My Pig." Frankie said.

As soon as Frankie walked in the front door Maria jumped up and hugged him. "Honey, where have you been? You're never home this late, I have been worried sick."

"Are you okay, son?" Antonio asked.

"Yes, Papa, I'm fine."

"Here, dear lad, sit down and eat your dinner," Nanny said.

While he ate his dinner, Frankie began to explain why he was so late.

"You did a good deed, son. Only one question: if My Pig followed you home where is he now?" Antonio said.

"I put him in the garden shed with a bucket of water. Can I keep him, Papa? Can I please, Mama? He's a beautiful little pig. He's snow white with big brown spots. And he has one blue eye and one brown eye."

Antonio looked at his wife and Maria smiled at him with an endearing look. "Well, I don't see any problem with keeping him. But when Farmer Bob gets home after Christmas you'll have to get his permission," Antonio said.

"This is so cool. I can take My Pig fishing with me, thank you, Papa!"

The next morning it took a moment for the numbers on Frankie's alarm clock to come into focus. Uh, it's 5:37 a.m., he thought.

Frankie jumped out of bed thinking of My Pig. As soon as he laced up his second shoe he grabbed his fishing pole and tackle and went running out to the garden shed. Inside the shed My Pig could hear Frankie coming and he began to oink with joy.

My Pig was so happy to be with Frankie that he ran circles around him on the way out to the grape orchard. Frankie started running and laughing as My Pig chased him playfully down a row of grape vines on the way to the pond.

"Welcome to my pond, My Pig. Now it's your pond, too. This is where we'll be fishing and playing," Frankie said.

My Pig ran around the pond looking everywhere, exploring his new home. He froze in his tracks when he saw his own reflection for the first time in the glassy water. He oinked a bunch of times, then looked up at Frankie.

"That's you, My Pig!" Frankie said.

A sunfish jumped out of the water and back into the cool liquid.

My Pig oinked and jumped up. Two sunfish jumped out of the water and back in and My Pig oinked and jumped up twice, once for each fish.

"Hey, you jumped for each fish. That must have just been luck," Frankie said.

My Pig watched and listened to his new master with enthusiasm.

"Watch me cast this worm into the water, My Pig. This is how we fish. Sometimes they hit immediately, sometimes they take a long time, and other times they don't bite at all. Papa once told me that's why they call it fishin' and not catchin'," Frankie said.

My Pig was having a blast at the pond. Frankie bent down and gave his new little friend a big hug. "My Pig, I'm glad you like the pond. We can play here all day today! Papa said I can take today off from school."

Frankie and My Pig fished and explored around the pond all day long.

"Well, it's time for dinner, My Pig. We have been here all

day. You must be hungry." They walked to the edge of the grapevines and, to Frankie's surprise, Calvin was walking down the road with his head hanging low and his hands in his jacket pockets.

"On no, stop, My Pig. Stay right here and don't move," Frankie said.

My Pig saw Calvin and made a low rumbling sound deep in his chest.

"Hey rich boy, it must be nice to go home to a nice family," Calvin said.

Calvin looked up at Frankie then kicked a stone down the road and kept walking.

"That was a close call, My Pig. Calvin is a mean bully. He seemed depressed or something this time. I've never seen him sad before. We're safe for now, at least. Come on, let's get home," Frankie said.

Frankie and My Pig had another surprise waiting for them at home.

"Wow, Look what papa built for you while we were at the pond, your very own pig pen! And he put the old doghouse inside the fenced off area for you!" Frankie said.

My Pig went inside his new home, drank some water, and ate from the bowls Antonio had placed there for him. The little fellow walked inside the old wooden doghouse, turned around and laid down, looking at Frankie with what seemed like a big smile.

"This is great! See you later, My Pig. Enjoy your new home."

Chapter Twelve

Frankie had a wonderful evening, but that wasn't quite the case for Calvin. Calvin called Chad.

"Come on, Chad. Answer your darn phone," Calvin said.

"Chad, it's me, Calvin."

"Hey dude," Chad said.

"Hey Dude, Frankie has a new pet pig and he's all happy. I saw him out on the road. Anyway, let's talk about that later. Man, Chad, I don't know, but this new girlfriend Dad has is putting a real number on him. She walks around the house wiggling her little behind and Dad does anything for her. She treats me like crap and Dad doesn't say anything to her. And, dude, check this out, she's swindling him into buying her a new Cadillac!" Calvin said.

"Buying her a Cadillac, with what money? Damn, Calvin, you need some new clothes and she's going to get a Caddy?" Chad said.

"Yep, and she makes these cheese ball dinners and acts like she's treating Dad like a king. My mom's dinners blew hers off the map. I miss my mom, I wish she was still here," Calvin said.

"Dude, let's practice baseball tomorrow after school," Calvin said.

Chad was relieved that Calvin changed the subject from his deceased mom. Calvin's mom died in a horrible car wreck on a dark and rainy night. She drove to the market to get just a couple items to complete the nice dinner she was making and she never returned. Her French sauce was still simmering on the stove. Calvin never saw her again.

"Yeah, we need to practice. It would be so great to win the first Christmas tournament for Walnut Street School. Let's do it, let's win Walnut Street's first trophy ever!" Chad said.

"I have an idea. We should practice every day after school. This way we will get so good we will win the game," Calvin said.

"Good idea, dude." Chad said.

"We need to get the team together every day and practice, practice, practice," Calvin said.

"Or, we need some new kid to move to town that is a home-run hitter," Chad said.

"Oh that's stupid, dude, we have good hitters. And you can't count on home runs to win a game. We need to constantly get on base. Then we need to bring our guys home one and two at a time, always advancing around the bases. I'll pitch a winning game so the other team can't score on us."

Chad agreed with Calvin so he wouldn't get upset. "Yes, you're right, Calvin. We can win with your plan and a lot of practice."

"Dude, let's mess up Rich Boy tomorrow. He seemed way too happy with his new little friend. We're going to get him tomorrow, you hear me?" Calvin said.

"I hear you, Calvin," Chad said.

Calvin heard yelling in the background on Chad's end so he hung up the phone. Chad's parents were always yelling at each other.

The next morning was a sunny but cool day. When the sunbeams made it through the oak tree at the bus stop they reflected off of Katie's copper-colored hair like a new shiny penny.

Calvin walked up to Katie and grabbed a lock of her hair.

"Red-headed Kate, your hair shines so nice in the sun I could almost kiss you," Calvin said.

Katie yanked her head away and said, "Yuk, not in a million years!"

Chad heard this and started teasing Calvin. "Calvin kissed Red-headed Kate! Calvin kissed her!" Chad said.

"C-Calvin k-k-kissed her?" Billy asked.

"Here comes the bus, you jackasses! Why do you hang around these two bullies, Billy? " Katie said.

"Hey, where's Frankie? We're going to get him good," Calvin said.

"Dude, maybe he's getting a ride from his sister in her Mustang convertible," Chad said.

"He's dead when we see him next," Calvin said.

The bus headed down the road while Mrs. Harrington went through the gears. "Next stop is Walnut Street School!" she said.

Anna was waiting for Frankie out in her car with the engine revving. Anna leaned out her window and yelled towards the house, "Come on, Frankie, we're going to be late for your doctor appointment!"

After Frankie got in the car he leaned out his window and yelled, "Bye, My Pig! I'll be back soon."

The 1965 red Mustang sailed down the dirt road with a purring smoothness.

"I love riding in your car, Anna, turn this song up!" Frankie said.

When Anna reached the paved highway she turned the music up for her brother. "There you go, rock out, Frankie!" she said.

Anna and Frankie were cruising and rocking out when a black hot rod caught up to them. The tough-looking hot rod stayed right along the side of them, revving its loud engine.

"Look over at them. What are they doing, Frankie?" she said.

"He's rolling down his window," Frankie said.

Anna grabbed the chrome handle, cranked down the window and looked right at the guy.

"Hey, little Miss Riding Hood, do you want to race?" the guy said.

The guys in the black car started busting out laughing.

Anna held her steady speed and gave them no indication that she was going to punch it. She slowly grabbed for the chrome stick shift lever on the floor of the car. She kept her cool and spoke softly to Frankie, "Hold on tight, Frankie."

As Anna gave the laughing guys a flirtatious wink she put the pedal to the metal.

"Wahoo!" Frankie said.

"Hold on, we're going to lose them at the on-ramp! Look back, Frankie, where are they?"

"They're still in their lane but they're catching up to us, Anna!"

Right when Anna came to the freeway on-ramp she yelled, "Hold on, Frankie!"

Their bodies leaned left when Anna turned hard right up the freeway on-ramp and left the guys in the black car in their tracks.

"Wahoo! We won! That was so cool, Anna! Was I a good enough copilot? Sometimes my mind can't react fast enough in emergency situations," Frankie said.

Anna nodded with a big smile on her face and stuck her hand up while she drove safely down the freeway. "You were a perfect copilot, Frankie!"

Frankie gloated with approval while he high-fived his sister.

Chapter Thirteen

My Pig was waiting in his pig pen as close to the gate as he could get. He had been watching for Frankie to come back ever since Frankie left. And sure enough My Pig saw the red Mustang coming up the road.

"Hurry Anna, pull in already," Frankie said.

"Jeez, guy, wait until I stop the car before you get out, you're going to hurt yourself," Anna said.

Frankie left the car door open and ran to the pig pen. My Pig started running in little circles. Frankie dropped to his knees in the dirt and hugged him.

"Hi, My Pig! I missed you. Let's go fishing!" Frankie said.

Anna giggled when she saw My Pig running around Frankie. "I'll get your door, Frankie. I'm going inside to see what mama's doing."

Maria always worried about Frankie's checkups at the doctor's office. With Frankie's brain imbalance she never knew what could happen. On Doctor Day Nanny always made a nice dinner to help ease Maria's worries.

That evening Nanny served the family prime rib *au jus* and twice-baked potatoes stuffed with fresh garlic, basil, and three cheeses. For a vegetable Nanny had winter squash that was fresh picked right from Maria's garden plus a serving of her homemade soup with farm fresh vegetables.

When everyone was seated at the table Antonio began to say grace. "Please bow your heads in prayer, everyone. Heavenly father, thank you for a good checkup today for Frankie and thank you for this food that we are about to eat in the name of God. Amen."

"Amen," everyone said.

"Oh, Elaine, this is a superb dinner you prepared," Maria said.

"Thank you, Madam," Nanny said.

Maria spoke with a smile. "Oh, Frankie, I am so happy the doctor said you are doing okay. He said that when you get a little older your memory should return and that your mentality should slowly catch back up to your age," Maria said.

Frankie looked slightly puzzled. "Thank you, Mama," he said.

"Pass the butter please, Anna. Oh, this is a wonderful meal isn't it, Antonio?" Maria said. "It's a beautiful evening. You know, Frankie, I visited with your new little friend, My Pig, and he's a sweet guy. He has a lot of personality. Would you like some more sauce on your meat, Antonio?"

"Please, honey," he said.

"You look lovely this evening, Anna," Maria said.

"Thank you, Mama," Anna said.

Frankie had been waiting for the proper time to speak. "Papa, can I go run some scraps out to My Pig before I eat my dessert?"

Antonio glanced at Maria in an exchange of smiles. "Sure, Son, go ahead."

Nanny started preparing a bowl of scraps for My Pig. "This is wonderful, Frankie," she said. "I can make use of our daily scraps instead of tossing them out. Do bring back my bowl, dear lad."

Frankie was so excited to see his little pig that he started to run out the door without the bowl of scraps.

Anna joked, "Did you forget something, Frankie?"

The family laughed as Nanny handed Frankie the bowl of

scraps like a quarterback handing off a football to the running back. Frankie leaped off the porch and sprinted to the pen yelling, "My Pig! My Pig! Look what I have for you!"

Balancing the bowl in one arm while unlatching the gate with the other, he ran into the pen so fast that he tripped over his own feet, sending the bowl of scraps flying in the air. He landed in the dirt with a thumping grunt and immediately broke out in laughter.

My Pig saw Frankie on the ground and food everywhere and went wild.

"Stop that, My Pig! Ha, ha, ha, stop licking me in my face, ha, ha."

Finally the little pig went for the food and Frankie was able to get on his feet absorbed in laughter. After gathering himself, he picked up the scraps, put them in the pig's bowl, and hugged his little four-legged friend.

"Woo, that was too much. I haven't laughed that hard in a long time, My Pig. I can't wait to see you tomorrow. Tomorrow after school I'll show you around the orchard. Goodnight, My Pig," Frankie said.

Frankie headed upstairs to his room feeling happier than he had in years. He had found a new friend. Looking down from the stairway at his family, he thought for a moment then spoke. "Good night, Papa. Good night, Mama and Anna. Good night, Nanny."

"Good night, Frankie!" they all said.

"Oh, and Papa, thank you for building My Pig's new home. And thank you, Nanny, for his scraps," Frankie said.

"You're welcome, Son. You have a good night sleep; we're all so happy for you," Antonio said.

"No, thank you, dear lad. It saves me a trip to the trash can!" Nanny said.

Frankie was falling asleep peacefully with the pitter patter of rain drops on his window and Christmas colors flashing on his walls from the Christmas lights outside, when he reached that state of euphoria that you sometimes feel when you're just entering a deep sleep.

The last thought Frankie had was about his little pig before his body twitched and he went to sleep.

Chapter Fourteen

Calvin was scheming an evil plan that night. Like a vampire out for blood, Calvin wanted Frankie. He picked up his phone and dialed Chad's number.

"Hello, Chad. It's Calvin."

"Hey, dude," Chad said.

"Dude, did you call Billy? Does he know to meet us at the oak tree tonight at 2 a.m.?" Calvin said.

"Yep, he knows."

"Okay, good, this is a perfect rainy night. They won't see us in the rain and under the darkness of the clouds. I'll see you at the tree," Calvin said and hung up.

Outside Chad's windows thunder roared and lighting flashed in the night.

Calvin was the first one waiting under the big oak tree at the bus stop. Chad arrived a few minutes later.

"Chad, is that you?" Calvin said.

"I hear you, Calvin, but I can't see you," Chad said.

Calvin said, "I'm here under the tree."

The two bullies met with cold wet high fives. The smell of wet soil and foliage filled the night air. Rain drops filtered down through the oak tree as thunder rumbled in the distance.

"Dude, it's pouring out here. Nice rain gear you have there," Chad said.

Chad noticed Calvin's face becoming solemn.

"Thank you," Calvin said. "It was my last Christmas gift from mom before she died in the wreck."

Chad became a little nervous when Calvin mentioned his

deceased mom. "Uh, where the hell is Billy?" he said.

"I don't see or hear him out there. Maybe he chickened out," Calvin said.

The night lit up like a giant camera's flashbulb when the lighting hit.

Chad started counting seconds to see when the thunder would follow. He figured every second represented the lightning being one mile away.

"One, one thousand, two, two thousand."

A pounding of thunder hit with a smashing boom.

"Two seconds, that lightning was only two miles away!" Chad said.

"I saw Billy! The lightning lit up the road. He's coming, and he's walking kind of funny, like he's bowlegged or something," Calvin said.

"Yep, that's him all right. Why is he walking so weird?" Chad said.

"I'm c-c-coming guys! S-s-s-sorry I'm late," Billy said.

Calvin and Chad broke out in laughter, pointing at Billy.

"What in the heck are you wearing, fool?" Chad said.

Calvin was laughing too hard to speak.

"It's a gl-glad b-bag. I have three s-s-sweatshirts on under it," Billy said.

"Look at his feet, what in the heck," Calvin said.

"I p-put a gl-glad b-b-bag on each foot and wrapped them up in duct t-tape," Billy said.

Calvin and Chad laughed at Billy for a while.

"Well, let's give him credit for showing up at 2 a.m. on a stormy night," Calvin said.

Calvin eyeballed each boy. "Ok, let's get started. Remember once we get there keep it quiet. Don't talk unless you really have to. Don't sneeze, cough, nothing. You both know your jobs, so do them right," Calvin said.

The three bullies prepared to tromp up the soggy dirt road in the wet stormy night. Calvin couldn't help from laughing at Billy one more time.

"Ok, fasten your hoods and zippers, and uh, your duct tape and let's go," Calvin said.

They tromped up the dark muddy road, their footprints vanishing in the rain. Rain poured on and off to the sound of eerie thunder. Lightning bolts flashed through the night.

After their sopping wet trek Calvin bent low and began to whisper.

"Okay, we're here, hunker down and keep quiet. Wait here until I wave you up and then man your positions," Calvin said.

Calvin was like a prowler in the night, peeping into the Vincente's windows. Crouching low he scooted to My Pig's pen.

The Vincente's residence was quiet other than rain dripping from the eves. The Christmas lights were turned off and only a soft light glowed from the front porch.

This will get rich boy good. I hope it ruins his Christmas, Calvin thought. When he made it to the pen he opened the gate, turned around and waved up Chad and Billy.

"Show time! Let's go, Billy," Chad said.

"I shouldn't of g-gotten s-s-suckered in in to this. Th-this is wrong. I'm g-going home," Billy said.

Chad looked furious as he shoved Billy.

"Too late now, stutter boy, move it!" Chad said.

Calvin waved them up again. "What are you idiots doing? Get up here!"

Chad and Billy crouched low as they ran to the pig pen, and were briefly revealed by a flash of lightning.

Chad manned the gate so that My Pig couldn't escape. Calvin and Billy walked up to the old dog house and looked in. The little pig was sound asleep on top of his blanket. It was easier than Calvin thought. He waved to Billy to stand back as he bent down and pulled My Pig's blanket toward him. He wrapped the blanket around My Pig and grabbed him like a big overgrown baby. Once he got a good hold of the sleeping pig, Calvin whispered, "Let's go!"

The bullies hustled down the road in the stormy night like three football players heading for the end zone. The storm had slowed and the clouds were breaking. Light from the moon flickered on and off. The bullies' footprints deepened in the wet mud.

"I'm getting tired, he's pretty heavy," Calvin said. My Pig grunted in his sleep.

"Shhh, quiet don't wake it," Chad said.

"I'll go about one hundred yards then you'll take the stupid pig, Chad," Calvin said.

Chad nodded and started getting psyched up for his turn.

Billy walked bowlegged with his glad-bagged feet as fast as he could. I wish I could just take off running for home, he thought.

Calvin couldn't last any longer. "Here, Chad, take him," he said.

Chad took the pig from Calvin's arms. "Damn, he's heavy," he said.

"You carry him for about half a mile then its Billy's turn," Calvin said.

Chad huffed and puffed. "It's cold and wet out here," he said. "This pig is reminding me of little pigs in a blanket with warmed syrup on them in my comfy warm home."

When My Pig heard Chad's voice he woke up and jumped

out of his arms like a coiled spring.

"Oh no!" Chad said.

The little pig came within inches of escaping but Chad was able to grab a hind leg before he disappeared in the night. The pig fought hard to get away but Calvin and Chad were able to contain him and put him back into Chad's arms. As My Pig squealed for help, Calvin took off his belt and fastened it around the blanket to secure him.

With My Pig contained the bullies continued on.

"I'm getting tired," Chad said.

"Billy, get ready," Calvin said. "Chad, hand the stupid pig to Billy."

"Here, Billy, take him!" Chad said.

Billy, feeling the weight of My Pig, said, "He's t-too heavy f-for me."

"Take him for just a hundred yards, Billy. You can do it!" Calvin said.

The moon went dark and it started to rain again. What a sight to behold, Billy huffing and puffing in glad bags, carrying a kidnapped pig with what looked like two slave drivers following him in night. Lightning lit up the road ahead in a surreal moment of bluish white light.

"There's the walnut tree up ahead! That's where we'll do it, behind the walnut tree in the old abandoned McCloskey barn," Calvin said.

Calvin carried My Pig for the final stretch. "Chad, open the barn door," he said.

"I got it, dude."

Calvin walked into the old barn holding My Pig like the Grim Reaper. He looked vicious as he yelled at the boys, "Get in here, Billy! Shut the door and latch it, Chad!"

Calvin untied the pig and tossed him onto the dirt floor.

My Pig slowly backed up, then looked up at Calvin and grunted at him like a bull ready to charge.

"Don't look at me like that, you stupid pig, or I'll cook you luau style!" Calvin said.

"We're n-not g-g-gonna h-hurt him are we?" Billy said.

"I'm thinking of killing him right now," Calvin said.

"P-please don't!" Billy said.

"Maybe we shouldn't kill him," Chad said.

Calvin looked at Frankie's pig with rage, debating it in his mind. "All right, all right, we won't kill the stupid thing. We'll just kidnap him for a while. We'll get Katie to feed him."

Billy let out a sigh of relief. "I'll f-f-feed him t-t-too," he said.

"Yeah, whatever, let's get out of here. Chad, make sure to shut the door and latch it so the pig can't get out," Calvin said. "One question. Billy, did the glad bag and duct tape idea keep your feet dry?"

Billy wiggled his toes around in his trash-bag covered shoes. "Uh, y-yep," He said.

Calvin and Chad busted up laughing on their way back out to the muddy road.

My Pig walked around the inside of the barn shaking his head from side to side. He pressed his head against the old wooden barn door and nudged forward on it, realizing it was latched. He laid down on the dirt floor of the creaky old barn and squealed for Frankie all night long.

Chapter Fifteen

Frankie woke the next morning as happy as could be. He was glad that Anna was giving him a ride to school that rainy morning. He sat on the Mustang's red seat with his hand on the chrome door lever yelling at the little pig's pen. "Bye, My Pig. I'll see you after school. Stay dry in the dog house!"

Rain drummed on the Mustang's soft convertible top while the windshield wipers swished in tempo. The metal dashboard and red carpet of the Mustang had a damp but pleasant odor about it on rainy days.

Anna took her driving more seriously than usual that day. "Buckle up, Frankie. It's a wet one out here."

The Mustang seemed to be handling the muddy road fine until its first slide to the left, then to the right and they were heading for the ditch. Anna went into emergency mode handling the car with an amazing amount of skill.

"Hold on Frankie!" She turned the wheel one way while slamming on the emergency brake then quickly releasing it and turning the wheel the other way, then punching the throttle. The shiny red Mustang stopped in the middle of the muddy road facing the wrong way.

"Woo, that was close!" Anna said.

Frankie's eyes widened, his hand cupped over his mouth in disbelief. "Good save, Anna! Where did you learn that?"

"An ex-boyfriend," Anna said. She turned the car around and they headed towards school a little slower while busting up laughing.

Calvin and Chad were under the oak tree waiting for

Frankie to walk up.

"Hey, here he comes in his sister's car. Should we pummel them with mud balls?" Chad said.

"No we've done enough for now," Calvin said. "He has to be missing the pig, let him stew in that."

"Hey, wait a minute. They're both laughing, Calvin, look!" Chad said.

Frankie and Anna were laughing so hard they didn't even notice that they had just passed Calvin and Chad at the tree.

Anna's mind went to Christmas when she and Frankie passed some small farm homes that were decorated. "Hey, I hope it stops raining tomorrow. Felipe is going to put up the giant Santa Claus and Christmas tree figures in the orchard up by the road," she said.

Felipe, who is from Italy, is Antonio's main grape grower and vintner. He lives in the one bedroom cottage in the grape orchard.

"Yahoo! The Christmas Eve party is almost here!" Frankie said.

The Mustang pulled up to the curb at the school and Frankie ran to class in the rain. He opened the classroom door and looked back at Anna with a smile, waving goodbye.

Frankie sat down in his seat in the classroom daydreaming with a happy aura about him. My Pig is waiting at home for me. I love My Pig, he thought.

By the end of class the sky was as blue as Katie's eyes. Frankie and Katie sat in the back of the bus in deep conversation. The yellow bus idled with a rumble before taking off.

"Oh Frankie, that's an awesome story. That is so cool that you saved this pig's life. And you have a fishing friend now. I am so happy for you," Katie said.

"Thank you, Katie, I love My Pig."

"And, wow, what a cool name, My Pig. Well, we're at the tree," Katie said.

"All out for the oak tree!" Mrs. Harrington said.

Calvin, Chad, and Billy were unusually quiet. They sneaked off the bus fast and disappeared.

Katie stepped off the lower step and looked behind her at Frankie. "I can't wait to see your little friend. Bye, Frankie!" Katie said.

"Bye, Katie, you'll have to stop by some day and see him!" Frankie said. He made his way home and ran up his driveway as excited as a kid in a candy score.

"I'm home, My Pig. I'll be right out, I have to go to the bathroom!" he said. Frankie ran up the curving stairs in a hurry, not paying attention to the aroma of fresh baked brownies. "Hi, Mama! Hi, Nanny!"

"Hello, honey," Maria said.

"Frankie, I have homemade brownies and French vanilla ice cream," Nanny said.

"Maybe later, thank you Nanny. I have to go play with My Pig," Frankie said.

Nanny and Maria looked at each other with surprise.

"He's never turned down your brownies, Elaine," Maria said.

"Uh, Madam, please refer to me as Nanny," Nanny said.

Maria giggled but didn't continue with the debate. "Elaine, do you think I should use all red Christmas flowers or add a dash of pink?"

"I think you should add at least some white flowers, and a small dash of pink," Nanny said.

"Oh yes, how silly of me, I have to pick the white poinsettias as well."

Frankie dashed for the front door with one thing on his

mind: My Pig. Before closing the front door Frankie looked over his shoulder to Maria and Nanny. "Bye," he said. He rounded the corner from the driveway so fast that he slid out, catching his balance on one hand and kept moving.

"I'm coming, My Pig!" he said.

Frankie got to the gate and ran to the old dog house and peered in. He froze in panic and yelled out for My Pig in distress. "My Pig, I'm home!" he said. He looked around in all directions then ran out of the pen yelling for his pig.

There were men on ladders in the back of the house installing more Christmas lights. Frankie ran up to one of them with a look of terror on his face and yanked on the man's jeans.

"Have you seen My Pig?" he said.

The worker looked confused. He looked down at Frankie and spoke in Spanish while shaking his head. "El cerdo?" he said.

Frankie stared at him for a moment, then sprinted frantically to the other worker named Juan. "My Pig, My Pig, have you seen him?" Frankie said.

"No, Frankie," Juan said.

Frankie ran around to the front of the house, his head turning left and right. He ran out to the road and looked up and down as far as his eyes could see yelling My Pig, My Pig at the top of his lungs. His heart pumped hard in his chest. His eyes widened with terror. Then he ran back to the pen, went inside and looked to the sky yelling, "My Pig, My Pig!"

Frankie fainted in the pig pen, landing in the mud.

Juan heard Frankie yelling and came running. "Frankie where you is? You in mud?" he said. When Juan picked Frankie off the wet ground he noticed the empty look in Frankie's eyes. Frankie seemed spaced out. "I love My Pig," he said.

"Amigo, help me with the boy!" Juan said. The other Mexican man gently set down the Christmas lights and got off his ladder and ran to Juan and Frankie.

Maria and Nanny were in the house when they heard the doorbell ring. They were shocked at what they saw. Juan and the other man were propping Frankie up with Frankie's arms over both their shoulders.

Frankie was muddy and his eyes seemed empty.

"Miss Maria, something wrong with Frankie," Juan said.

"Oh my gosh! Please, Juan, you and your friend please get Frankie up to his room so Nanny and I can clean him up," Maria said.

Anna heard the commotion and came running down the stairs. One look at Frankie and she knew what it must have been. Anna ran out the door dashing for the little pig's pen.

My Pig, you're gone! Where did you go? You would never leave Frankie, something is fishy, she thought.

Juan and his friend helped Frankie sit down on his bathroom chair and left the house.

"Thank you, Juan," Maria said. "Elaine, I'll get him out of these dirty clothes. Please go get me some towels so we can clean him up."

"Yes, Madam," Nanny said.

Maria looked in to Frankie's eyes and saw a blank stare. "Honey, look at me. Are you okay?" she said.

Frankie didn't answer.

"Frankie, tell me what happened," Maria said. Still there was no answer.

When Nanny came back in with the towels Maria looked at her with a dropped jaw and wide eyes. Nanny knew right away there was something wrong in Frankie's brain.

Once they got Frankie into his pajamas and in bed he

stared blankly at the ceiling and mumbled, "I love My Pig." Then he fell asleep.

Anna came running up the stairs worried sick about Frankie. She knew from taking him to his doctor appointments that the neurotransmitters in his brain could be affected from any relational stress. "Mama, I know what's wrong with Frankie. It's My Pig. He's gone, he's not in his pen. He's nowhere around."

Maria looked puzzled. "My Pig ran away?" she said. She immediately called Antonio at the packing shed. He was with Felipe putting grape jams in cases to be shipped out.

"Yes, honey, that's right, My Pig is gone and Frankie is terribly affected. I'm very concerned, Antonio," she said.

Antonio felt the seriousness in his wife's voice and went into action.

"Felipe, we have a little problem. Frankie's pet pig has run away and Frankie is very upset. You know his brain is delicate," Antonio said. "Please get on the CB radio and call the whole crew to meet me here right away."

"Yes sir, I'm on it," Felipe said.

Antonio and Felipe stood out in front of the packing shed waiting for the orchard workers to arrive. Antonio had his arms crossed with one hand on his chin and Felipe's thumbs stuck out of his jeans pockets like a cowboy waiting for action. One at a time the pickup trucks pulled up to the shed.

Felipe spoke in his slight Italian accent. "Antonio, what's Frankie's pig's name?"

"He simply named him My Pig," Antonio said.

"Okay, we're looking for My Pig," Felipe said.

"Let the guys know that it is very important. They must look all night if they have to."

"Yes sir, Antonio," Felipe said.

Felipe got the crew of workers there fast. "Okay, Antonio, they are all here now. I will organize a structured search party. We will do whatever it takes to bring home My Pig," Felipe said.

"Thank you, Felipe, I know you'll do a great job," Antonio said. He patted Felipe on the shoulder and headed for the house to care for his family. Maria ran to him in tears and hugged him tight.

Antonio embraced his wife, saying, "Don't worry, honey. I've sent out a search party for My Pig."

"Frankie doesn't seem right. Something has happened in his brain," Maria said.

"Where is he now," Antonio said.

"He's sleeping in his bed. He wouldn't even talk and his eyes looked glassed over. All he did was mumble, "I love My Pig,"

"This is a real shame. Poor Frankie. Hopefully, the guys will find My Pig by the time he wakes up," Antonio said.

Chapter Sixteen

Night had set in and the Vincente Christmas lights were glowing outside with Christmas cheer. Inside the beautifully decorated home was a different story. It was time for dinner.

"Should I go up and wake Frankie, Mama?" Anna said.

"How much more time until dinner, Elaine?" Maria said.

"I can serve dinner in half an hour, Madam."

"Let's wait ten more minutes, and then go wake him for dinner, honey," Maria said. "I'm very worried about him."

My Pig was locked up asleep in the old McCloskey barn. He dreamt Frankie was slipping into the pond in quicksand and needed his pig to save him. All of a sudden My Pig woke up and ran full speed ahead for the old barn door. When he slammed it with his head the door moved a little but didn't open. The little pig oinked loudly and ran around the barn thinking of an escape plan. He had to get to Frankie; he could sense something was wrong with his master.

"Mama, I'll wake up Frankie now for dinner," Anna said.

"Thank you, dear."

Anna walked into Frankie's room and turned on the light. "Frankie? Frankie, are you okay?" she said.

Frankie was sitting up in his bed staring at the ceiling in silence. He didn't even acknowledge Anna. Anna was terrified for her brother.

"Uh, Frankie, dinner is ready," she said.

Finally Frankie looked at her. When Anna saw his blank stare she tried to hide her bewilderment. "Nanny made your favorite lasagna, Frankie," she said. "Come down and eat dinner now, we are all waiting for you. Felipe and the whole crew, all the workers, are out searching for My Pig. Papa told them to search all night if they have to. Don't worry, brother, they'll find him. Come down and eat, you need to keep your strength up."

Frankie just sat in bed repeating over and over with an empty stare, "I love My Pig, I love My Pig."

Anna ran downstairs, shocked at Frankie's behavior.

Outside Felipe was working hard with the orchard crew. He was sitting in his pickup truck in front of Frankie's house when he got on his CB radio to contact Jose, the assistant manager of the orchard workers. Jose was from Mexico and could communicate well with the orchard workers. "Jose, are you out there? Jose, this is Felipe; come in. Come in, Jose," Felipe said.

The radio made scratchy sounds before Jose came in. "Señor Felipe, this is Jose. Come in."

"Jose, call all the men and tell them to meet me in front of the boss's house on the road, pronto."

"Si, Felipe, over and out," Jose said.

Felipe sat in his truck out on the road with his lights on and engine running. He could see headlights coming toward him from all directions. Jose was the first one there. He got out of his truck and spoke to Felipe.

"Oh, Señor Felipe?"

"Yes, Jose, what is it?"

"What is the name of the peeg," Jose said.

"My Pig," Felipe said.

"Oh, it's your peeg?"

"No, Jose, it's My Pig that we are looking for."

"Oh I see, Señor Felipe; we are looking for your peeg."

"No, no, Jose! We are looking for Frankie's pig!" Felipe said.

Jose stood outside Felipe's truck scratching his head. "What about your peeg, Señor Felipe?" he said.

"I don't have a pig!" Felipe said.

"I am very confused, Señor Felipe, because you said we are looking for your peeg." Jose said.

Felipe got out of his truck, took off his cap, and slapped Jose on the head with it. "Jose, listen closely. I don't have a pig. Frankie named his pig, My Pig!" Felipe said.

"Oh, I see now," Jose said. "We are looking for *Frankie's* peeg, his *name* is My Peeg."

"Yes!" Felipe said.

The two men started slapping each other with their caps, then broke down in laughter.

All the other trucks showed up and Felipe made a better plan to find My Pig. "Okay, everyone listen up, here's what we're going to do. Let's drive in organized lines spread out. First we'll comb the entire orchard and if the pig is not in the orchard we will start at the far end of the road and search all the way up to the school," Felipe said. "Let's stay organized this time and not get separated. Turn on all your spotlights and we will search all night if we have to. This is very important for Antonio. These are orders from headquarters, men, let's move out!"

The family was in the house trying to eat dinner amongst their worries.

Antonio took charge. "If Frankie wants to stay in bed and skip dinner then we'll let him sleep. Maybe he will sleep off the shock and be better for breakfast. I know we are all worried for him but we need to eat and keep up our energy for Frankie." Antonio continued with grace before dinner. "Please bow your heads. Dear Lord, please help us to find My Pig and please be with Frankie and help him through this. Thank you for this food that we eat in the name of the Lord, amen."

"Amen," everyone said.

That night everyone went to bed not realizing Frankie was staring out his window at the searchlights going through the orchard. He kept saying, "I love My Pig, I love My Pig, I love My Pig." Frankie finally fell asleep to the sound of trucks rumbling through the night.

Felipe drove up the road towards the school, searching with his spotlight. Why does that darn raven keep swooping down towards my truck and then flying ahead of me? It's like the bird is trying to tell me something, Felipe thought.

Felipe held the black CB microphone in the palm of his hand. "Jose, this is Felipe. Any sign of My Pig? Over."

"Señor Felipe, this is Jose. No sign of My Peeg. Over."

The CB radio crackled so Felipe hung it up.

Trucks were combing the land with spotlights shining through the orchards and toward the school late into the night. Men's voices with Spanish accents could be heard calling out for My Pig.

My Pig was running around the old barn oinking and squealing as loud as he could. He heard the trucks and men calling for him, but they couldn't hear him. He passed out from squealing all night, limp as a noodle.

Felipe headed back to his little one-bedroom cottage home in the orchard next to the packing shed. "I'll leave a note for Jose in front of the coffee pot in the shed. He'll see it first thing in the morning," he said.

Felipe's note read: "Jose, please continue the search party for My Pig first thing this morning. I have to ship some cases of grape jam to New York. When I'm finished I will join you on the search. Good job! Thank you."

Chapter Seventeen

Before falling asleep, Felipe thought about My Pig. Nanny said that you never want to leave Frankie's side. Why would you run away, My Pig? Felipe thought.

The next morning Jose was up before the sun rose pouring his first cup of coffee while reading Felipe's note. "I will start right now to find My Peeg," Jose said.

Jose drove slowly through the orchard with one hand on the wheel and one hand holding his coffee mug. He looked around while sipping his coffee. "I will find you, My Peeg, and I will be the hero of the Vincente's," he said.

Jose was driving through a row of grape vines when he thought he was seeing things. A lady dressed in a business suit walked out from the row of grape vines, startling him, and he threw on his brakes. What the heck, I almost dropped my coffee in my lap, he thought.

The lady walked over to Jose's door with a confident sense of authority.

"Good morning, sir. I am Mary Winthorp, Channel Seven News," she said.

"Oh, si, I have seen you on the TV!" Jose said.

"Sir, people have called us saying they saw unusual activity last night. Trucks seemed to be searching for someone with spotlights all through the night. Voices were heard yelling for someone. Sir, is there someone missing from the Vincente family?" she said.

"Yes, Mrs. Mary. There is someone missing."

"Sir, has anyone called the police to file a missing person's report?"

"The Policia? Oh, no, Mrs. Mary. It is only the family's pet peeg that is missing." Jose said.

Mary Winthorp took notes as Jose spoke. "Are you sure, sir? Can I have your name, sir?"

"Will I be on the TV like a movie star?"

"I might be able to get you on TV, sir."

"Yes, Mrs. Mary. My name is Jose. I am the manager of the orchard workers here at the Vincente's."

"Are you sure there are no persons missing, sir? Is anyone from the Vincente family missing? Are the women safe?"

"No, Mrs. Mary, there are no peoples missing," Jose said.

"Okay, that's enough for now, Jose. Thank you for your time and have a nice morning," Mary Winthorp said.

Jose rolled up his window and continued searching for My Pig. He looked over his shoulder and saw Mary Winthorp getting into a news van and heading up the road.

"I am a star of the movies!" Jose said.

A man named Dave drove the Channel Seven News van up the dirt road with Mary Winthorp in the passenger seat taking notes.

"Dave, this guy Jose said they were only looking for the Vincente's pet pig. I think there is more to this story. I think there may be some kind of foul play. Maybe someone is missing or even dead," she said.

Dave waved his hand through the air. "Oh, I don't know, Mary, this is farm country. Maybe you're stretching it a bit here. I don't think you have a story on this one," Dave said.

Mary Winthorp shook her head, "No, there's a story here, I can feel it," she said.

Inside Frankie's house Anna was the first one up. Still in her pajamas, she sipped tea while looking out the window. Where are you, My Pig? Felipe would have called by now if they had found you. Where are you? She thought.

Nanny entered the room looking concerned. "Good morning, dear Anna. I hope Frankie eats his breakfast."

"Good morning, Nanny. I hope he's better today, I'm worried sick. I hope My Pig returns," Anna said.

"Me too, dear, I know how serious this can get," Nanny said. While Nanny prepared breakfast she kept looking out the kitchen window hoping to see My Pig basking in the morning sun in the front yard. No such luck, she thought.

Antonio and Maria came downstairs a little later and the family sat at the breakfast table getting ready to wake Frankie.

"I'll go get him," Antonio said.

"Good luck, honey. Please bring Frankie down to eat. Please tell me he'll be okay," Maria said.

"He'll be okay, honey," Antonio said.

Antonio knocked on Frankie's door and called out for his son. When Frankie didn't answer Antonio walked in. Frankie sat up against his headboard staring straight ahead with empty eyes in silence.

"Good morning son, it's time for breakfast. Frankie, Frankie do you hear me? Son, it's time for breakfast," Antonio said.

When Frankie didn't answer, Antonio realized something was seriously wrong with his son. He walked over and sat on the bed next to Frankie.

Frankie stared into emptiness, not looking at his papa. Antonio wrapped his arms around him and spoke to him from his heart.

"Son, I know you're hurting. Sometimes we lose loved ones and it hurts. I know how much you miss him but, Frankie, you must not give up hope in finding My Pig. We will find him but I need your help. I need you to eat and keep up your strength," Antonio said.

Antonio didn't know if his son could comprehend what he was saying. He knew from the looks of Frankie that the stress had caused something to happen in his brain. Frankie was becoming sick with sadness.

Although Antonio felt sad for his son when Frankie burst into uncontrollable crying in his arms, he was glad to see some type of emotion other than a dead stare. He held Frankie tight.

Frankie tried to say "I love My Pig" but only a gurgle came out.

"It's okay, it's okay, son, let it out. I'm here for you," Antonio said.

For a moment Frankie seemed to snap back. "Papa help me, something is wrong," he said. Then he sat back against his headboard and went in to a dead empty stare again.

Antonio grabbed his shoulders. "Frankie, Frankie!" he said. "Okay, son, you must be down for breakfast in ten minutes. Listen to your papa, son. We are all waiting for you at the table. I will see you in ten minutes," Antonio said.

Deep concern for his son filled Antonio's mind on his way down the curving stairway.

Maria was waiting with open arms in the living room for Antonio.

"I wish I had better news, honey. Frankie doesn't seem right. I told him we are all waiting for him at the table. I told him to be down for breakfast in ten minutes. Let's all sit down and wait for him to come downstairs," Antonio said.

"More tea, Anna dear?" Nanny said.

"Yes, please, Nanny."

"And you, Madam."

"Please, Elaine."

"Sir, some more coffee?"

"Yes, Nanny, thank you," Antonio said.

Maria said, "Antonio, honey, Felipe called while you were with Frankie. He said he was very sorry but after an exhaustive search the guys could not find Frankie's pig. They even tried baiting him with a truck load of corn. Felipe and Jose checked this morning and nothing, nothing but coyote tracks and some torn up corn cobs."

Anna and Nanny looked at each other thinking the same thing. Coyotes, did the coyotes get the little pig, they wondered.

"Listen up, please, everyone. I want us all to be hopeful, positive, and strong for Frankie. We will find My Pig," Antonio said.

"But he needs to eat, Papa," she said.

"I know, Anna, I know," Antonio said.

Frankie held it until his bladder was about to burst, but finally he had to get up and go to the bathroom. He almost collapsed when he stood up. He was getting weaker, he needed food. Due to his bout with spinal meningitis, Frankie needed to eat three healthy meals plus a snack or two every day. And he wasn't eating at all. He balanced himself on one knee with one hand holding on to the windowsill. Then he walked to the bathroom.

Taking a deep breath, Antonio stood at the bottom of the stairway. With one foot on the first step he looked up at Frankie's door that seemed a mile away. The family was counting on him to get into that room and get Frankie down to the kitchen to eat. One more deep breath and Antonio headed up the stairs, turned the doorknob and walked into Frankie's room.

Frankie was lying on his side under the covers, looking away.

Antonio said, "Hello Frankie," but Frankie didn't answer. "Frankie, it's your papa." Still no answer. "You need to get your strength to help find your little pig. You must eat and remain positive so we can find him. He knows your voice, Frankie, you need to call out for him. You can't just lie in bed. We need you. My Pig needs you. You need to help find him and bring him home," Antonio said. "You are a Vincente. You must be strong, eat and prepare to search for My Pig like a strong man! We will start by getting some food in you. And then we'll figure out the best strategy to bring him home."

Antonio hoped he was saying the right words while he went to Frankie's closet to get his robe. "Sit up, son, and put on your robe," he said. Finally, Frankie pushed off his bed and stood up, reaching out an arm to slip into his robe. "That's it, my big man," Antonio said.

Then Frankie's knees buckled and he fell into his papa's arms. Antonio felt the weakness in Frankie's body. This is not good at all, he thought.

"Frankie, you need to stimulate the oxygen in your blood. You need to exercise in fresh air. The first thing you need is food. Put one arm around me and let's go," Antonio said.

He felt a brief sigh of relief when Frankie put an arm over his shoulders. With arms around each other Antonio started to guide Frankie away from his bedroom.

"You got it, son! You can do this, Frankie!" Antonio said.

Step by step they made it to the doorway when Frankie panicked. He grabbed on to the doorknob not wanting to leave the security of his bedroom.

"Come on son! It's okay. Be a strong man and get to the table and eat!" Antonio said.

Frankie held on to the doorknob with all his might while Antonio held him, prying him away from the door.

"Frankie, we are going down the stairs now. Take a look. Do you see the stairs, son? We will take one step at a time. Gather your strength and let's get to your breakfast," Antonio said. "I'm right here, Frankie, holding you all the way. That's it, one step at a time. Let's show mama we can do this. Next step now, that's it."

Maria heard them on the stairway. She walked to the foot of the stairs. Antonio looked down the stairs and saw his wife standing there with her hand over her mouth crying. He waved her away.

Frankie was looking down at each step and he didn't notice his mama crying. Maria went back to the dining room crying silently and telling Anna and Nanny that Antonio and Frankie were coming down the stairs.

Anna put a hand on her mama's arm, giving her a look of endearment and said, "It will be okay, Mama."

"Oh dear, here he comes, I'll warm his plate," Nanny said.

"Good job, Frankie, you're doing very well. Let's continue to the next step now," Antonio said.

When Frankie stepped onto the first floor a feeling of accomplishment flowed through his bones, giving him a boost of energy.

"Good morning, Frankie!" Anna yelled out.

Nanny quickly dished out Frankie's breakfast.

When Maria saw Frankie enter the room her tears turned to a smile. The three ladies started clapping for Frankie. They cheered him on as Antonio sat his son down in his dining chair.

"Thank you for warming my coffee, Nanny," he said.

Nanny went right to work.

"Dear Frankie, here's your favorite breakfast. You have farm fresh eggs, your favorite country sausage and English muffins that you love to spread with your papa's grape jam," she said.

Antonio looked at Maria with a concerned look.

"Frankie, eat your breakfast and gain your strength back like the strong man that you are. Just start with one small bite of your eggs. Then take your time eating until you finish everything," Antonio said.

Frankie's eyes roamed over each item before picking up his fork. He noticed Nanny had already spread the grape jam on his English muffin. I usually do that myself, he thought. With the first bite, Frankie's taste buds kicked into gear and he started shoveling food into his mouth with a shaky fork.

"Take your time son," Antonio said.

Everyone was full of joy watching Frankie taking in nourishment.

"Good job, brother!" Anna said.

Antonio made a gesture for everyone to continue on as normal. The three ladies understood.

"Would you like some more tea, Madam?"

"Please, Elaine," Maria said.

"And tea for you, Anna?"

"Yes, please," Anna said.

Anna grabbed an English muffin and spread her papa's grape jam on it.

"Yummy jam, Papa," she said.

"Thank you," Antonio said.

Frankie kept eating although his pace had slowed.

"More coffee, Sir?" Nanny said.

"Just a warmer," Antonio said.

Just as Nanny started to lift the coffee pot from the stove, joy turned to terror. Frankie's fork fell to the floor as he choked, dry heaved, then choked again.

Antonio jumped up grabbed Frankie out of his chair and ran him to the bathroom. Frankie continued with the dry heaves, gasping for air, his heart pounding overtime while he stood over the toilet with Antonio holding him up. The dry heaving didn't seem to stop.

Anna stood outside the bathroom door listening in. Maria and Nanny stood in the kitchen embracing each other in fear.

Frankie's dry heaves finally stopped and a gush of vomit filled the toilet. With a big gulp of air and an arching of his back, he continued vomiting for what seemed like forever.

By the time Maria burst into the bathroom crying out Frankie's name, Antonio was holding him in front of the sink. With water dripping from Frankie's quivering chin, Antonio dried his face.

"I'm proud of you for eating, Son. Put your arm around me, let's go sleep for a while in the guest room so you don't have to climb the stairs," Antonio said.

The worried family gathered in the living room looking at each other for answers. Antonio anxiously paced back and forth while he thought of what to do for his son. Then he put wood in the fireplace and started a warm fire.

"We need to call the doctor," Anna said.

"She's right, I'm calling him right now," Maria said.

After speaking to the doctor and gaining some direction Maria hung up the phone and went back to her family to explain.

"What did they say?" Anna said.

"The doctor said we need to give Frankie one cup of water every hour. He said to just let him sleep right now and try a bowl of soup for dinner. He said to keep him very warm with lots of blankets. And, if he doesn't eat by tomorrow morning to call him back for the next step," Maria said.

"I'll help you, Mama. We can do shifts through the night," Anna said.

"Oh, honey, I would be too worried to sleep anyway, but thank you, Anna. It will help me knowing you're all getting your sleep. I will sleep next to Frankie's bed and give him his water every hour. Don't worry I'll be fine," Maria said.

❧❖❧

The three bullies waited for Frankie at the bus stop like laughing hyenas hanging out around the tree. Calvin and Chad were snickering at the thought of seeing Frankie walking to the bus stop full of sadness missing his little pig.

"He's usually here by now. Where is rich boy? Billy, get out on the road and yell when you see the bus coming. Come on, Chad, let's hide. We're going to pulverize rich boy this morning," Calvin said.

After hiding behind the bushes for some time and Frankie not showing up, Calvin started to flare at the nostrils. "Where is he? Damn it!" he said, then started pacing back and forth kicking stones. "See him coming yet, Billy?"

"N-nope no s-s-sign of h-him," Billy said.

"That piece of garbage. I'll kill him! He's supposed to be coming up the road by now!" Calvin said. Picking up a stone, he heaved it at Billy out on the road, just missing him.

"What w-was that f-for?" Billy said.

"Shut up, you stuttering fool!" Calvin said.

"H-here c-comes the b-bus! And, K-Katie is r-r-running up the r-road," Billy said.

Calvin picked up a thick oak branch the size of a baseball bat. His mind unleashing a fury, he stared down Billy and Chad with crazy eyes.

Billy and Chad froze in disbelief. Calvin walked over to

the big oak tree and yelled at it as if it were Frankie standing there looking at him.

"Don't look at me like that, rich boy!" Calvin said. The first swing of the branch connected at face level on the big tree trunk, making a cracking thud. Before swinging again Calvin yelled out, "I said stop looking at me like that, rich boy!" Calvin swung the branch with a crazy rush of adrenalin. Then, he just kept swinging again and again while looking up at the sky through the tree branches and screaming.

Chad and Billy stood next to each other, frightened, as splinters flew everywhere.

When Calvin's branch had broken down to a spiky stub he held it in his hand like a knife and turned with a crazy spin. His fiery eyes stared right through Chad and Billy and in a cruel whisper he said, "You idiots. I'll have your necks."

Mrs. Harrington pulled up to the giant oak tree in a cheerful mood and opened the double doors. "All aboard!" she yelled. Billy ran to the back of the bus with Katie and sat down. Over their heads it read, Emergency Exit, in big red letters.

Chad and Calvin sat up front. "Dude, are you all right?" Chad said.

"I'll be Okay," Calvin said.

Billy leaned in close to Katie and told her everything. He told her that they kidnapped My Pig and that he didn't really want to be a part of it but he was scared. He told Katie that he and she needed to feed and water the little pig.

"That's why Frankie isn't here today. Oh my gosh, he must be devastated," Katie said.

The yellow school bus approached the school. "Next stop, Walnut Street School! This is your last day before Christmas vacation!" Mrs. Harrington yelled out.

All the kids on the bus clapped and cheered, except for the three bullies and Katie.

"I know Frankie better than anyone at school. I know this is hard on him this time, really hard. Billy, I'll feed My Pig until he's put back at Frankie's where he belongs," Katie said.

"Okay, Katie, th-thank you," Billy said.

That evening after school Katie opened the old McCloskey's barn door and walked in. My Pig was bouncing up and down on his front legs, grunting, acting like an attack dog.

Katie bent low holding her hands out, her red hair almost dragging in the dirt.

"It's okay, My Pig, I'm Frankie's friend. I'm here to help you. Here, have some of this corn for now and here's some water," Katie said.

My Pig was puzzled to hear Frankie's name and be given food and water by a strange girl, but he felt comfortable with Katie for some reason. He approached the corn with caution. Katie put her hand on him and petted him with love.

"That's a boy, My Pig, don't worry, I'm your friend. Those darn bullies will kill me if I take you home. Don't worry, I'll make sure you won't be here long. Goodnight for now," Katie said.

When Katie shut the old wooden door My Pig tilted his head to the side. He heard something different that time. He heard the sound of a chain bouncing a couple times before settling on the outside of the door. It didn't make that kind of sound when the bullies latched it, the pig thought. He went over to the door listening to Katie's footsteps crunching the leaves as she walked away from the barn. When he didn't hear her anymore he leaned on the barn door and felt it give a little more than it did before. My Pig lay down facing the barn door with a full belly and fell asleep.

It was just a few days until Christmas. The kids were on Christmas break, the annual Christmas fair was being set up at the fairgrounds, and holiday cheer filled the valley while Frankie slept in the downstairs guest room, sick with sadness.

Antonio was pacing back and forth in the living room. The Christmas Eve party is in two days and it's Frankie's favorite night of the year and he's sick, Antonio thought. We can't cancel the party. Some of our guests are traveling all the way from Europe and the Governor is coming, the mayor is coming, a famous actress and actor are coming from Hollywood. We cannot and will not let them down. Oh, My Pig, where are you?

Antonio stared at Nanny in thought then raised his hands in a confident gesture. "Nanny, continue your party preparations, the show must go on! We will find My Pig and Frankie will be well," he said.

Nanny decided she must help by being positive and cheerful. After all, the Christmas Eve party was her favorite night of the year as well. She loved being the boss and teacher of the assistants she had hired. Nanny perked up at attention with a smile.

"Yes sir! My three assistants will be here in about two hours and of course Charles our Butler in internship will be here on Christmas Eve promptly one hour before the party starts.

I'll share a secret with you sir, Charles may be ready for me to crown him as an official butler this year."

"Charles has been a great butler for us, Nanny. Now, we just need to find My Pig so Frankie will heal. I'm going to wake him now and take him up to his room," Antonio said.

"I pray for dear Frankie, sir," Nanny said.

Antonio and Frankie, papa and son, arm in arm, stepped

up the long curved stairway.

"That's it son, just keep your arm around me and keep climbing one step at a time. Great job, Frankie! That's it, hop into your bed now. You'll be more comfortable in your own room. I'll wake you for dinner and your mama will be up shortly to pour you a glass of water. Make sure you stay hydrated son," Antonio said.

Looking at Frankie for a moment before closing the door, Antonio became very concerned that his son wasn't talking to him and that his eyes had a look of emptiness.

"Get some rest, Frankie," Antonio said.

After Antonio closed the door, Frankie started saying, "I love My Pig, I love My Pig," over and over to himself.

Chapter Eighteen

Evening was settling in and the first star appeared in the sky. Frankie was thinking of My Pig and My Pig was thinking of Frankie.

My Pig was getting more and more frustrated, more and more anxious to get to Frankie. Memories started spinning through his head like a tornado. He envisioned waking up in Frankie's arms after being saved, and then a picture of the pond went through his mind, then of him chasing Frankie through the grape vines.

My Pig's head was low and his eyes were opened wide. He stared at the old barn door like it was a predator that he must kill before it killed him. Then like a bolt of lightning he flew for the barn door, connecting head first with a sound like thunder in the night.

The old barn door opened like a shot and then closed again. Its rusty old hardware squeaked and creaked in the old wood. My Pig backed up again and headed for the door, and boom! He hit it square in the middle and it opened and quickly closed. Again and again he hit the old door but didn't break free. All he achieved was a sore head. He walked in a big circle, his head aching. Then as calm as could be, the pig just walked over to the door until the entire side of his body was pressing against it. He stepped a few inches more into the door feeling it flex out a little. He stood there for awhile, holding his position and pressing against the door.

Then he applied more of his weight on the door and he could now see out through the crack in the door. The crack got a little wider. He was tiring but he didn't want to give up. I must get to Frankie, he thought.

Suddenly the door made a popping sound and gave outward a little more. My Pig leaned in and pressed with all his might and then he heard another, "pop, pop!" sound. To his amazement the last two screws flew out of the rusty latch sending the door flying open and My Pig flying out with so much force that he did three complete rolls before landing on his back.

The little pig was so excited to be free from the old McCloskey barn that when he went to get up on his feet, he panicked and scooted quickly for cover. He ducked into a thick bush where he laid down and fell asleep. After some time passed, My Pig woke up. He listened for footsteps or voices, but he only heard the quiet of the night. He poked his head out of the bush and looked around. The moon lit up the night and stars twinkled bright in the clear skies.

He got out of the bush and quickly walked around the barn and out toward the road. Frankie I'm coming home, My Pig thought. He was tired and sore and drained, but he was happy to be going home to Frankie. He was so exhausted he could hardly see straight. But he knew that as soon as he reached the dirt road it wouldn't be long before he would be home. Then, finally, there was the road and he became so happy and excited to get to Frankie that he forgot all about being tired. He was running down the dirt road as happy as a puppy escaping from the pound.

My Pig was heading home to Frankie when a pickup truck with its bright lights on appeared out of nowhere heading right for him. The bright lights blinded him and he froze in his tracks.

The truck came to a stop and a man got out. It was farmer

Bob, the local pig farmer, with his white hair, his bushy white beard and his blue-jean overalls covering his big jolly belly. He stood between his truck and My Pig illuminated by the bright lights.

"What in the dickens, a pig frozen still in the middle of the road?" Farmer Bob said.

He was able to walk right up to My Pig and just pick him up. He took the pig over to his truck and put him in the back, then closed the tailgate. He headed for his farm home which was the opposite way from Frankie's.

My Pig was at the back of the truck looking toward his home at Frankie's with tears in his eyes and squealing. Farmer Bob turned on the light in the back of the truck and looked at the pig through his rear window. "Wow! That's a nice looking pig," he said. "Hi, buddy, you've got one brown and one blue eye and beautiful markings. And you have perfectly shaped ears. I'll be darned, I think you could win at the fair."

Farmer Bob had raised hundreds of pigs and he didn't realize that My Pig had originally come from his farm. He shut the back light off and My Pig rode down the road in the dark.

Chapter Nineteen

At Frankie's home Nanny and her three lady assistants were busy doing the preparation work for the Christmas Eve party. They were putting together hors d'oeuvres and special treats for the guests as well as parts of the main dinner course they'd be serving.

Nanny loved the big walk-in cooler that Antonio let her use out in the packing shed. The party cake had been delivered and placed in the cooler by the bakers. It was a big beautiful three-level cake that smelled of vanilla and peppermint. It had edible Christmas trees and snowflakes and a gingerbread house with edible ornaments on it.

Nanny was in her happy place directing her assistants around with cheer. One assistant was cleaning dishes in the kitchen sink when she noticed the Channel Seven News van slowly driving by the house.

They seem like they're filming the Christmas decorations, one of Nanny's assistants thought. The Vincentes are a bit famous around here after all. Maybe I'll get noticed by Hollywood, maybe I'll be on TV, the assistant thought. She looked in a mirror running her fingers through her hair wondering if she was beautiful before getting back to polishing the silverware.

Frankie, on the other hand, was sleeping and getting worse. He needed to eat to regain his strength. Maria was asleep in Frankie's chair that she had pulled next to his bed. She was due to wake up in fifteen minutes to give Frankie his hourly glass of water. Maria didn't realize yet that something was wrong, then her motherly instinct woke her up. She shook off her exhaustion, then focused on her son. Her face turned to a look of horror.

"Frankie! Antonio, get in here, Antonio, come quick!" Maria said. She was shocked to see Frankie going into massive convulsions. Through her terror she let out a high-pitched scream. "Honey, honey!" she said.

Antonio knew something was terribly wrong when he burst into the room.

"He's having seizures, I'll call an ambulance!" he said. Antonio's heart beat hard in his chest as he ran down the hall urgently to dial the emergency hospital's number. Kicking into survival mode Antonio conquered his fear and kept as calm as he could to help his son.

He raised the phone to his ear and spoke with authority saying, "This is Antonio Vincente and my son Frankie is having convulsions. Get here immediately!"

Maria was trying to hold Frankie steady as he convulsed and shook like mad. The terror on Maria's face was frozen in time.

Frankie was convulsing so hard that half of his body would rise above the bed then slam down. His eyes were rolling into the back of his head. His bed was making awful rattling noises. He shook, quivered, and flopped around on his mattress, showing only the whites of his eyes.

"They're on their way!" Antonio said.

Antonio heard a voice in the hallway. It was Anna. She didn't know what was going on until she walked into Frankie's room. Then she let out a scream. "Lord have mercy! Somebody help us!" Anna said.

"Where are they?!" Maria said.

When the paramedic's ran in to Frankie's room and

injected the long thick needle into his thigh, spurting blood, it was like a dagger going in to Maria's heart. Frankie's body stretched out and stiffened, then shook and relaxed. His eyes closed, then reopened in a show of glazed hazel that started to clear. He took a deep breath then looked at the paramedics in wonder.

Maria cried with relief in Antonio's arms. Antonio looked over his shoulder at the Paramedics. "Thank you, you just saved my son's life," Antonio said.

The paramedics looked at Antonio and Maria with satisfied smiles, "You're very welcome," they said. They left the room, then returned with a rolling hospital bed. They strapped Frankie in the bed and carried him down the stairway and into the ambulance.

Frankie watched the Christmas lights in a daze while the driver pulled away onto the dirt road. The ambulance led the way with its red lights flashing in the night. Frankie was tied down in the bed with a paramedic and Maria at his side.

"Lift your head please, Frankie, I'm putting this oxygen mask on you to help you breathe some nice fresh air," the paramedic said.

Maria, with tears in her eyes looked out the back of the ambulance through the small square window. Comfort warmed her when she saw Antonio and Anna following in the Suburban. She saw her Christmas lit home glowing as it faded in the distance, with Nanny peering out the kitchen window, waving in tears.

Maria raised her hand, waving back. "Pray for him, Nanny," she said.

Anna was looking in the passenger side mirror at a van that was following them.

"The Channel Seven News van is right behind us, Papa,"

she said.

"Yes, that's annoying," Antonio said.

The ambulance, Suburban, and the news van all drove in a single file down the dirt road passing farm houses lit up for Christmas and the holidays. Camera flashes came from the news-van like shooting stars from the night sky.

Mary Winthorp, the reporter, gave her driver Dave a snappy look. "I told you we have a story here, Dave," she said.

"You're a gifted reporter, Mary," Dave said.

In the back of the ambulance Maria felt better to have Frankie in good care and she prayed for him to heal and find happiness.

Under the oxygen mask, Frankie mumbled, "I love My Pig." But no one heard him.

Chapter Twenty

Frankie laid in a hospital room with an IV needle in his arm for hydration, dripping to the beat of the beeping monitor. Under an oxygen mask he slept sedated from medication. Antonio, Maria, and Anna stood over him praying.

Antonio shook his head. "I can't believe this pig running away has hurt Frankie to this point. I know My Pig is a special little pig. But is he that special to put Frankie in this condition?" Antonio said.

"I think it's more than what we can see, Papa. Frankie told me recently that all he wants is a friend to fish with at the pond and he just wants to be able to play baseball with the other kids. I sense there might be some bully problems at Walnut Street School, but Frankie has never said anything about being bullied. You see, Papa, that little pig became Frankie's fishing friend," Anna said.

"I see. Yes, that does make sense, Anna. I guess sometimes we can't see what others are experiencing. Maybe we only see what's on the surface because we are lost in our own selfish thoughts. Maybe, just maybe I need to get out of my own little brain and reach out more to my family with my heart and learn what they are feeling deep inside," Antonio said.

"That's beautiful, honey. That would be a wonderful thing to do. But, my good husband, this is not your fault," Maria said.

"No, it's not your fault, Papa," Anna said.

Putting his hands on the ladies' shoulders with a smile, he said, "You are two wonderful women."

"Maria, I want you to come home with us now. The nurse said that Frankie will sleep all through the night. He's in good hands now and we all need to rest so we can be strong for him tomorrow," Antonio said.

Maria raised both hands in front of her saying, "Oh, honey, I couldn't. It would do no good anyway because I would be too worried about Frankie to sleep. You and Anna go home and rest. See if Nanny is okay and put some food and water in My Pig's bowls so when he finds his way home tonight he can eat. We must stay positive. Oh, Anna, please change Frankie's sheets on his bed. Nanny is too busy preparing for the party. I'll have the nurse bring me a cot. I'll be right here by Frankie's side. Go on now, don't worry. I'll be more content here," Maria said.

Antonio knew his wife well. He knew she would be staying with Frankie so he gave her a hug and kissed her goodnight. "Okay. Try to get some sleep, Maria," he said.

"Goodnight, Mama," Anna said.

Maria stood, waving goodbye with a positive smile.

"Frankie will make it home for Christmas. The Christmas Eve party is his favorite time of the year," she said.

Antonio and Anna drove home in the Suburban over the dark dirt road in deep thought. "There's something special about Christmas decorations in the countryside," Anna said.

"Yes, the homes look nice," Antonio said. "You know, Anna, I was thinking, My Pig always waited for Frankie to get home, and he followed Frankie wherever he went. That little pig loves Frankie like no pet I have ever seen in my lifetime. It's like he's attached to his belt loop. So then, why, why would My Pig run away? It doesn't make sense."

"I was thinking the same thing, Papa, it doesn't make sense," Anna said.

Chapter Twenty-one

The bullies had no idea how much pain they had caused. So many others were feeling Frankie's pain: his family, Nanny and her assistants, Katie, Felipe, Jose, the other orchard workers, and Frankie's doctors. So would about a hundred Christmas Eve guests who would soon find out, as well as Mrs. Harrington and Mr. Conte. The list of people who would be affected by the bullying goes on and on. And the only thing the bullies were thinking about at the time was their own pride in winning at the annual baseball game at the Christmas morning fair.

Calvin was sitting on his bed slapping a baseball into his glove while going over in his mind the pitches he had been practicing with the team. My sinking ball will work on the taller batters and my killer curve ball will strike out the shorter hitters, Calvin thought.

Throwing off his glove with the baseball in it, Calvin turned on his little black and white TV and leaned against his headboard, crossing his arms and legs. What he saw on his TV made him leap off his bed.

"That's Rich Boy's house!" Calvin said.

Mary Winthorp, the reporter, was going live. "I am here at the Vincente grape orchard in the San Joaquin Valley where the famous Vincente purple grape jams and juices are produced. Grape farmers have been on the hunt for someone who is missing. Actually, the missing someone is a pet pig named My Pig. My Pig is very close to seventeen-year-old Walnut Street School student, Frankie Vincente. Vincente has brain damage after contracting spinal meningitis and his doctors with his parent's consent have put him back in the ninth grade with a goal of exercising his brain back to his normal level of mentality," she said.

"Since his pig went missing, Frankie Vincente has been hospitalized and is in critical condition. He hasn't eaten in two days. If Vincente doesn't eat soon he could literally die from heartache. Vincente went into convulsions and was rushed to the hospital. He is currently being fed through an IV and he's breathing through an oxygen mask. According to a Walnut Street School student, Frankie Vincente loves to play baseball. He has always dreamed of playing in San Joaquin's annual Christmas Fair game, but he's been bullied out of it.

"The Vincente family needs to re-connect their son Frankie with his beloved pet pig. If anyone knows the whereabouts of the pig with one brown eye and one blue eye, and a white body with big brown spots, please call 555-505-1212. This is Mary Winthorp signing off, San Joaquin Valley Channel 7 news."

The ringing phone startled Chad out of bed. "Yeah. Hello," he said.

"Chad, it's Calvin, wake up! It's all over the news. It's about Rich Boy and his missing pig! They showed his house. They said he misses My Pig so much that he hasn't eaten and he's in the hospital and he can die!" Calvin said.

"What the..." Chad said.

Calvin yelled at Chad before hanging up the phone. "Call Billy and get to the barn right now. We're going to sneak the damn pig back to Frankie's!"

Chad had to wonder if he was dreaming at first, then he came to his senses, realizing the gravity of the news Calvin had told him, and he became so nervous that he could barely get dressed. After calling Billy, he fumbled his shoe laces a few times before finally getting them tied, and then sprinted outside for the old McCloskey barn. Chad ran into the night scared for his life.

Billy ran down the dirt road, a nervous wreck with fearful thoughts of going to jail for murder and at the same time praying for Frankie to be okay. Fr-Frankie d-doesn't d-deserve this. He would n-never hurt a f-fly. He c-can't help it that h-he's r-rich. He d-doesn't even know the d-d-difference b-between rich and poor, Billy thought.

Calvin's heart was pounding with fear so hard it seemed to propel him down the road. The only thing that gave him hope was thinking he and the other bullies could just put My Pig back home at Frankie's and they would be off the hook.

Chad and Billy both arrived at the old barn property at the same time. "Billy is that you?"

"Y-yes Ch-chad it's me."

"Did you see the news?"

"N-no I d-didn't."

"Something isn't right here. I didn't see it either. And where's Calvin? Come on, Billy, let's go in the barn and get My Pig. Maybe Calvin is setting us up for a prank or tricking us somehow," Chad said.

When Chad and Billy approached the barn, the door was opened and the inside was faintly lit by moonlight reaching through cracks in the old ceiling.

Calvin looked like a demon in its dark creepy home ready to trap its next victim.

"Where in the hell is the pig?" Calvin said.

Chad and Billy looked at each other in horror.

"Damn it, Billy, you were supposed to be taking care of him! Where in the hell is he?" Calvin said.

"I d-d-don't know! R-Red H-headed K-Kate was f-f-feeding him," Billy said.

"Kate, huh? Okay, that makes sense. She probably felt sorry for rich boy and his stupid pig. I bet she put the dumb pig back at Frankie's. Come on, idiots, let's go to Frankie's to make sure the pig is in its pen," Calvin said.

"It was on the news then," Chad said.

"Yes, it was all on the news, you fool! They said if Frankie doesn't eat he could die! We got to him so bad, he quit eating! If we get caught we could go to jail for the rest of our lives!" Calvin said.

The bullies walked down the dark dirt road in petrified silence to Frankie's house.

The moon beamed into My Pig's pen giving the boys a view right into the old dog house that My Pig slept in, and it was empty.

Billy and Chad became very scared. But Calvin had a weird gloat about him. Looking around at the Vincente's home all beautifully decorated for Christmas, Calvin sneered and laughed as he spoke.

"Well, I guess kidnapping the pig worked good. We got rich boy real good on this one. Let's get out of here before someone sees us," Calvin said.

Billy had an unusual look about him as he spoke. "I d-didn't w-want this to happen." He looked up at Calvin in disgust and then turned like the wind, running so fast that Calvin or Chad didn't even try to catch him. Billy ran home in the night scared to death of going to jail.

"I've seen Billy nervous a lot, but I've never seen him so scared," Chad said.

Chad crossed his arms across his chest and looked at Calvin for answers. "I'm scared too, Calvin, what are we going to do?" he said.

Calvin knew he had to come up with a plan. "Dude, let's meet at the old McCloskey barn tomorrow morning, say at 11:00 so we can sleep in a little. We'll track the pig and find him, then return him to the Vincentes and they will think we're heroes," Calvin said.

Calvin felt he had a smart plan. He got a big grin and his eyebrows rose into a crinkled forehead. "Maybe they will even pay us reward money!" he said. "We have all day tomorrow to search for the pig. And dude, after dinner don't forget we have our final practice game before the big day. I'm going to win the first trophy for Walnut Street School, wahoo!"

Chad couldn't believe Calvin was actually happy about anything during such a critical time with Frankie in the hospital and My Pig missing and it all being on the news.

"Okay, see you at 11:00 at the old barn," Chad said.

Chapter Twenty-two

The sun shined through the cool air on the day of Christmas Eve, Frankie's most happy time of the year and he was lying in a hospital bed hooked up to IV's. The hurt and stress of My Pig missing had caused the neurotransmitters in Frankie's brain to become chemically imbalanced and his mind inlayed with confusion.

Maria was waiting for the Nurse to come into the room and check Frankie's vitals and serve him breakfast. While praying that Frankie could go home for Christmas Eve, Maria heard footsteps coming to the door. To her surprise it was Antonio and Anna. Maria stood up with a smile and embraced her husband. Anna hugged her tired mama at the same time.

"The nurse should be in here any minute," Maria said.

"Sweetheart, you need to get some sleep," Antonio said.

"Yeah, yeah, forget about me," Maria said.

"How is he, honey?" Antonio said.

"He slept better last night than he has in days," Maria said.

"Good, join me in prayer," Antonio said. "Dear God, please let Frankie be better now, so he can come home for Christmas. Please Father, it is his favorite time of year."

"Amen," they all said.

Anna had her eyes closed and head down, feeling faithful in God. She could smell the scent of pine from the Christmas tree back at the house and she wanted Frankie to be there full of Christmas joy.

"Sometimes we don't understand God's powerful way of thinking. We must have faith in his will," Antonio said.

The door opened and the day shift nurse entered with a welcoming smile and carrying Frankie's breakfast tray. "Good morning," she said. She gently shook Frankie's shoulder but he just let out a snore. So she let him sleep as she checked his vitals.

Maria waited anxiously as the nurse wrote something on Frankie's chart. She hung the clipboard on the hook on the door, and turned to Maria with a soft smile saying, "He's improved. He needs his sleep now, so I won't wake him just yet. I'll be back in about an hour to give him his breakfast."

Maria, Antonio, and Anna celebrated in silent joy.

Before the nurse got all the way out the door, Frankie sat up and blared out, "Dinner, it's time for dinner!" Frankie shook his head trying to gather himself. He looked confused and lost as he spoke. "I'm sorry I'm late for dinner, Mama," Frankie said.

Antonio put his hand on Frankie's shoulder and spoke, "It's okay, son, we are all right here with you."

The nurse brought Frankie his breakfast in a hurry. Frankie grabbed his fork and started eating. "Breakfast foods are fun to eat for dinner sometimes," he said.

Maria and Anna hugged each other with joy. "How's the food, brother?" Anna said.

"Good, Sis, you should have Nanny bring you a tray."

"I think I'll wait until later, Frankie."

"Anna, are you giving me a ride to school today?"

Anna looked at the shiny hospital floor trying to figure out what to say, and then she raised her hand with her palm up and leaned her head towards Frankie. Smiling, she said, "You're now on Christmas break, Frankie. There's no school today. You need to eat your food and rest and then eat again in a few hours or so. You need to get home, Frankie. It's

Christmas Eve!"

"What, it's Christmas Eve?" Frankie said. He rubbed his head in confusion, his eyebrows squinted tight. "Anna, it's Christmas Eve! Let's get ready for the party!"

Frankie finished all his breakfast and laid back to rest. He needed to keep his food down. If he didn't the nurse said they would have to put him in intensive care. The nurse came back into the room and changed Frankie's IV bag and grabbed his breakfast tray.

"I gave him some more medication in his IV. This will knock him out until lunch. I'll be coming in and out checking on him to make sure he's okay," she said.

"Thank you so much," Maria said.

After the nurse left the room Antonio spoke. "Maria, I insist you get some rest now. Anna and I will be right here watching over him."

Maria nodded then laid down on her cot and fell asleep.

About thirty minutes had passed and the nurse walked in to see Frankie in a deep sleep. She checked his vitals again. "Wow, he seems as if he's improving by the minute. All his vital signs are back to normal. He seems to be keeping his food down this time too," she said. "I'll bring him a snack in an hour. Frankie's improving."

She did a silent golf clap with her hands close to her chest in her own little way, and then left the room.

Frankie turned over in his bed and let out a loud burp. The Vincentes jumped up to see him sleeping as if nothing happened. "Oh my gosh, that scared me," Maria said.

Anna couldn't help herself and let out a giggle. "I guess he likes the food," she said.

Just then the nurse walked back in with her squeaking white shoes and approached Frankie. She was relieved to see that he didn't vomit. She took his vitals and looked up at Maria. "He seems to be fine. I didn't expect all his vital signs to be back to normal, but sure enough, they are all normal. I think he is keeping his food down now and he's improving quickly," she said.

Maria smiled big, raising her hands in the air. "Thank you, Lord!" she said.

The nurse looked at the exhausted Vincentes. "I think you should all go home and take a break, then you can come back to have lunch with Frankie."

"Oh, I couldn't do that," Maria said.

Antonio agreed with the nurse. "Honey, you must come home for a few hours and take a nap in your bed. Frankie is in good hands and besides, I can tell he won't be waking up before lunch. He's out like a light."

"Papa's right, Mama," Anna said.

Maria, tired but concerned, looked at Frankie sleeping in the hospital bed. "Well, I suppose he'll be okay. And, I do need to be ready for the party tonight just in case I can make it," Maria said. She bent down and kissed Frankie on the forehead while he slept. The Vincentes left the hospital, piled into their big white Suburban, and drove for home.

Once on the road, Maria fell asleep in the passenger seat. Anna was in the back seat listening to music with an ear plug while Antonio drove wondering where My Pig could be.

When they arrived home they saw a few extra cars in the driveway. Nanny's servants were there preparing for the Christmas Eve party.

"Honey, we're home. Wake up and get into your own comfy bed," Antonio said.

"Okay, dear," Maria said.

The tall oak door opened and Nanny appeared with a

welcoming smile, waiting to see Frankie get out of the car. When Nanny realized Frankie wasn't there, her smile turned to a solemn look. She ran off the porch to greet the family and give Maria a hug.

"Hello, Madam," Nanny said.

"Oh my dear Elaine, it's so good to see you," Maria said.

Nanny ignored Maria calling her by her name that time. She grabbed Maria's hand and led her into the house. Charles the butler in training handed Maria a cold glass of lemon water.

"Oh, thank you Charles," Maria said.

"Anything for you, Madam!" Charles said.

Maria looked around her home admiring the Christmas décor. "Oh, Elaine, the house looks wonderful," she said. Then, sipping her lemon water, she walked up the grand stairway and retired to her room.

"It sure looks like Christmas," Antonio said.

"It looks fantastic, Nanny!" Anna said.

"Sir, how is he?" Nanny said.

"He's doing much better. He kept a meal down and they have him full of nutrients and vitamins. If he keeps his lunch down, we're expecting a fast recovery," Antonio said.

"Jolly good news, Sir, jolly good. Frankie loves the Christmas party," Nanny said.

Antonio tilted his head with a warm smile, "I know he does."

A couple hours had passed by when Nanny heard her phone ringing. The busy Nanny scooted around the kitchen into her maid's quarters. She picked up her antique phone, a bit out of breath. "Hello, the Vincente residence," she said.

When she found Antonio, he was standing at the Christmas tree admiring the family ornaments. Nanny tried her best to keep her professional composure though she wanted to burst out in joy. "Sir, I have a message from the hospital."

"Yes, Nanny?"

"Sir, Frankie's nurse has suggested that you and Madam should stay home and rest up for the party. Frankie has improved after keeping his breakfast down. The doctors are doing some advanced treatments as we speak. Frankie is getting some steroid and protein treatments and mineral solutions. They are being fed to him intravenously. After the treatment he will rest a while before having lunch. The nurse said that Frankie will feel very warm for a while but he should gain extra strength. Sir, she also said that the doctor will be calling you later this evening to let you know if you can bring Frankie home," Nanny said.

"This is great news! Frankie might make it for the party after all!" Antonio said.

Antonio held Frankie's favorite Christmas ornament as Nanny walked away singing "The Little Drummer Boy."

"Don't worry, Son, you'll be home soon."

He let the Santa fisherman dangle from its branch until finding its resting place. Antonio inspected the rest of the ornaments that were perfectly hung. He nodded in approval then went and poured himself a glass of his own homemade red wine. Sipping his wine Antonio looked out the kitchen window and wondered about My Pig.

Nanny and her assistants were right on schedule for the party. She gave her assistants a break and told them to come back in a few hours to begin the festivities. Soon after the assistants went on their break, Nanny's phone rang.

"Hello, Nanny, this is Frankie's nurse. I have great news. Frankie can come home for the Christmas Eve party!" she said.

"Oh this is wonderful, you just made everyone's Christmas!" Nanny said.

"Frankie told me all about his pet pig and what has happened. I think the best cure for Frankie would be to find his little pig," the nurse said.

"Yes, nurse, I know. I know you're spot on about that. Thank you for the most wonderful news. I will inform Mr. and Mrs. Vincente," Nanny said.

Tell them they can pick him up at six o'clock. Merry Christmas, Nanny!" the Nurse said.

"Merry Christmas to you, too! And, thank you for your great care!"

Once Antonio received the news, he thanked God, then immediately took charge. "Nanny, Maria and I will leave for the hospital before any guests arrive for the party. You and Charles greet the guests. Explain to them what has happened to Frankie and all about his pig. We will bring Frankie home sometime after six o'clock. I want you to have the guests prepared to welcome him with joy—uh, have them applaud or something. This should help take his mind off of his pig for the time being at least," Antonio said.

"Great idea, Sir. I shall carry out your plan with precision," Nanny said.

Antonio went upstairs to his bedroom to tell Maria his plan.

Grabbing his wife by her shoulders, he looked into her eyes. "Honey, I have great news, Frankie is coming home." Antonio said.

Maria peered into Antonio's eyes, stunned at what she just heard.

"Yes, Dear, you heard me right, we pick our boy up at

6:00. We are bringing Frankie home for the party!" Antonio said.

A tear of joy fell over Maria's shining smile. "Thank God, Our prayers have been answered!" she said.

"I have instructed Nanny to prepare the guests to welcome Frankie with a standing ovation upon our arrival," Antonio said.

"Oh, that's a great idea," Maria said.

At the hospital Frankie was dozing. Fluids from the IV bags were dripping into his arms. News of the famous Vincente child being in the hospital dying from sadness for his missing pet pig was starting to spread through the valley. Frankie's nurse was in the hallway telling the doctor Frankie's story.

"Yes, I saw that on the news. I hope Frankie is reunited with his little pig," the doctor said.

Chapter Twenty-three

The Vincente's drive to the hospital to get Frankie was the happiest Christmas drive they could remember. Antonio swung the big Suburban into the hospital parking lot and parked. He held the lobby door open for his wife and daughter. "After you, ladies," he said. When they got into Frankie's hospital room the first thing they noticed was that Frankie's face had a healthier glow.

Anna stood behind the nurse, looking around her into Frankie's sleeping face as the nurse bent over Frankie.

"Frankie, hello, Frankie, time to wake up," the nurse said. She shook his shoulder as she spoke, "Time to wake up, Frankie," she said again. Still Frankie didn't respond.

"Son, we're all here. Wake up, Frankie. It's Papa," Antonio said. Still Frankie didn't wake. Antonio turned to Maria with a puzzled look.

Then out of the blue Anna began to chant Frankie's rhyme, "Gonna catch a trout I have no doubt." Antonio and Maria joined in, "Or maybe it's a bass I pull out of class," they said.

Frankie stretched his arm over his head and arched his chest, half yawning and half singing in a distorted voice, "Cat fish, cat fish, put you on my dish," he sang.

Maria practically leaped upon Frankie, hugging him.

"Hello, son!" Antonio said.

Anna and the nurse were jumping up and down, hugging each other in joy. Anna walked over to the window looking out to the world with her arms raised up, "Merry Christmas!" she said.

Maria looked into Frankie's eyes. "Honey, you're coming home," she said.

"Okay, Mama," Frankie said.

Antonio leaned over Frankie with a big smile. "Son, guess what day it is?"

"Uh, what day is it, Papa?"

"Frankie, my boy, it's Christmas Eve!" Antonio said.

Frankie perked up when he heard it was Christmas Eve.

Anna stood at the end of Frankie's bed and shook his foot. "Come on, Frankie. We have to go to the Christmas Eve party!" she said.

Frankie sat up in his bed searching for words. "The Christmas Eve party is tonight?"

"Yes, Frankie, and everyone's coming to see you," Maria said.

"Wahoo! I love the party. We must hurry and get ready then," Frankie said.

At that, everyone in the room including the nurse, celebrated in joy, cheering for Frankie. "Yes, wahoo! Merry Christmas!" they said.

"Son, I brought your favorite Christmas outfit. Stand up now and let's get you showered and dressed." Antonio said.

"Yes, Papa."

Antonio grabbed hold of Frankie's arm and helped him out of bed. Frankie put an arm around Antonio's shoulder and they walked to the bathroom. Antonio opened the door and started to walk Frankie into the bathroom.

"Papa, I'm a big boy now. I'm in the ninth grade. I can go in by myself," Frankie said.

Antonio held his laughter to a low chuckle. "Oh, of course, son. What was I thinking? You're a big ninth grader, how silly of me. We'll be out here waiting for you," Antonio said.

While winking at his wife and daughter, Antonio said, "Frankie is back."

Maria and Anna wiggled with smiles as the nurse left the room. The Vincente's waited for Frankie to the sound of the running water.

Antonio grunted when he boosted Frankie into the back seat of the Suburban. "That a boy," he said. The Vincente family was on their way home. They were happy the Christmas Eve party was taking Frankie's mind off of My Pig.

Cars were parked up and down the dirt road and all over the Vincente's property.

As Antonio drove up the driveway through the beautiful cascade of trees, Frankie felt engulfed in Christmas lights and decorations. Looking all over the grounds, Frankie was full of joy. "Rudolph the Red-nosed Reindeer" just finished playing on the car radio. Antonio parked and opened his door. "All out for the Vincente Christmas Eve party!" he said.

Frankie was very happy, yet he felt drained. After a pause for a deep breath, he headed up the front porch with his family, one step at a time. Stopping for a moment, he held onto the porch pillar with his head down. Antonio's hand reached out, patting his son on the back. "Are you okay, Son?"

"Yes, Papa, I'm okay." Frankie made it to the top step and walked onto the porch. The solid oak doors opened and there stood Nanny and Charles. Everything seemed surreal to Frankie. He saw Nanny's big welcoming smile.

"Hello, dear Frankie, all your friends are here to see you," Nanny said.

Nanny seemed to him like a good fairy in a dream, waving her arm, calling him inside in slow motion. Frankie shook his head a little and headed for the smiling Nanny.

"Frankie, Merry Christmas!" Charles said. With a white

gloved hand he flipped on a switch, lighting up the great room. And then, to Frankie's surprise, all one hundred guests yelled out, "Surprise, Merry Christmas, Frankie!" Frankie lit up like a ray of sunshine. All the guests lined up to greet him. They presented him with gifts and hugs and kisses. Frankie was absorbed in a wave of love that seemed to never end. After Frankie had a chance to visit with everyone, the guests mingled amongst each other, enjoying the party.

With his arm around his happy son, Antonio walked Frankie upstairs to his bedroom. Frankie had socialized, eaten, and laughed with the guests. He couldn't have been any happier, for the time being. Frankie forgot how worn out he was until he reached the top of the stairs.

Charles, Nanny, and the three assistants started clapping. They were facing Frankie and Antonio from the foot of the stairs. Smiling guests applauded and cheered for Frankie sending a warm rush of goodness flowing through his chest. He took a deep breath with his hand over his chest, and then raised his other hand in a big wave, looking down to the great room. "Thank you! Merry Christmas!" Frankie said.

Amongst the cheering, Antonio and Frankie disappeared into Frankie's room.

"Wow, Papa, look at all the gifts I have in my room!"

"Yes, son, you sure are a lucky boy. We'll open them in the morning after we open our family gifts. But always remember, the best gift of all is love."

"Yes, Papa, God loves me."

"Yes, he does. Good night, Son, and don't forget to say your prayers."

"Good night, Papa,"

Down at the party Nanny walked by a few of the guests and overheard them speaking about her and Maria. The three ladies gossiped while sipping champagne.

"Maria calls Nanny Elaine. And Nanny insists that she refer to her as Nanny. They have been at this debate for years," one lady said.

"Nanny calls Maria Madam, and Maria insists that Nanny call her Maria," another lady said.

"Do you think they will ever end their debate?" the other lady said.

Nanny couldn't help herself. She walked up to the three ladies and said, "I'm the correct one, girls."

The three ladies sipped their champagne, giggling. One of the ladies patted Nanny's back with a long black-gloved hand and said with a smile, "You're the best Nanny in the land!"

Antonio was so happy that he chose that time to make a surprise announcement. He started clanging a spoon on a champagne glass to get the guest's attention.

"Everyone, may I have your attention please. I have a special announcement to make," Antonio said. First I want to thank you for coming to the party and for giving Frankie a grand welcoming."

"Wouldn't miss it for the world," a guest said. Cheers spread throughout the great room while Antonio continued speaking.

"I have a surprise to announce. Maria and I haven't told anyone yet. You're the first to know. Of course you all know of our Vincente jams and grape juices. Now, I would like to personally announce our new expansion of our grape growing endeavor. Maria and I are thankful to announce that we have produced our first estate bottle of Vincente Champagne!" Antonio said.

Just then, Charles, followed by Nanny's three assistants walked in the great room towards the guests with silver trays holding sparkling glasses of the Vincente's first pouring of their champagne and some sparkling grape juices.

"Bravo!" said one the guests, followed by cheers and applause from all.

Smiling faces and curious hands grabbed for glasses of champagne and some the sparkling grape juice. As soon as all the guests had their glasses raised, Antonio proposed a toast.

"Here's to a Merry Christmas, happy holidays and a wonderful New Year to all!" he said.

Everyone raised their glasses saying Merry Christmas and happy holidays. Compliments filled the room. The Vincente Champagne was a hit with the guests.

Chapter Twenty-four

While the Vincente's Christmas Eve party went on with holiday cheer, the bullies sneaked onto the fairground's baseball field. Most of the Walnut Street School team was there. The ball field was where the big Christmas morning game would take place the following day at the annual San Joaquin Valley State Fair.

Calvin and his team were lucky that the well groomed ball field was brightly lit while maintenance crews tested and worked on the lighting systems. Calvin stood on the pitcher's mound looking around at his team. "C'mon guys, man your positions! This is our final practice before the big game! I'm the pitcher who will bring Walnut Street School its first trophy! We will all go down in history!" Calvin said.

Chad stood up, took off his catcher's mask, and yelled, "Play ball!"

That's what the team had been waiting to hear, and they cheered and hooted across the lit up ball field.

Calvin eyeballed the batter then drew back his arm and let the ball fly. The batter swung hard and missed. Two pitches later the batter was struck out.

Chad stood up behind home plate and threw the ball back to Calvin. "Keep this up, Calvin, and we'll win tomorrow!" he said.

Calvin adjusted his cap and found his footing. He looked down, pondering. I'll be the first pitcher to win this game tomorrow, he thought.

The next batter got to home plate and raised his bat. The

baseball left Calvin's hand slicing through the night air heading for home plate. The batter swung and connected, sending the baseball over the center fielder's head. The fielder ran back for the ball while the batter rounded first base and landed on second base with a jump.

"Woo, nice hit!" the center fielder said.

Everyone clapped, including Calvin.

"We need good hits like this tomorrow, guys. Keep it up!" Calvin said.

Billy did a great job at short stop. He caught ground balls and threw out the runners at first base. He was catching pop flies on the run.

Practicing for the big game helped to take the bullies' minds off of going to jail for what they did to Frankie. After a long practice the players went home to get rested up for the big day.

Chapter Twenty-five

The Vincente's annual Christmas Eve party went very well. The last guests were leaving while Nanny's assistants kept busy cleaning up.

Frankie ate a big dinner and was asleep.

After a fun night looking beautiful in her red party dress, Anna went to sleep.

Antonio was in his bed trying hard to stay awake so he could give his loving wife a goodnight kiss.

Maria grasped the handrail of the curved stairway and put her tired foot onto the first wooden step looking forward to a good night sleep.

Nanny saw her and scooted to the stairs. "Madam, excuse me."

"Yes, Elaine?" Maria said.

"I would like you to join me for a moment in the kitchen. I know you must be exhausted, Madam, but I think you'll enjoy witnessing this special moment," Nanny said.

"Oh, Elaine, what is it?" Maria said.

Sticking her hand out, Nanny winked at Maria and Maria grabbed Nanny's hand and followed her to the kitchen. Maria's eyebrows lifted in wonder when she saw Charles and Nanny's assistants waiting for her in the kitchen.

Nanny presented her three assistants with their paychecks and thanked them for a job well done. Smiles of relief filled the room. Nanny stood with perfect posture looking at Charles. "Charles, I must discuss your internship as my butler," she said.

Charles tried to hide his nervousness.

"You have given much effort to your work. Yes, yes, you've had things that needed work, but you've corrected them," Nanny said.

Charles stood like a knight in front of his queen, listening to Nanny's serious tone.

"This year, Charles, you've proven your ability to take charge when needed. You showed me you can provide superb service. And this year you showed me you can perform your duties with proper etiquette while remaining in control in all situations," Nanny said.

Charles hid his anxiety that felt like butterflies in his stomach. Then, when he saw Nanny smile, the butterflies flew away. He watched Nanny's lips moving like in a dream. And he heard the words he thought he would never hear.

"I believe, Charles, that you could be a butler in the highest of palaces. There is only one thing left to do," Nanny said. Then she walked over to the butcher's block while Maria observed with tired but curious eyes. On the butcher's block sat a silver plate covered with a silver domed lid. Nanny nodded like a queen and two of her assistants scurried over and picked up the silver plate and took it over to Charles.

Charles didn't know what to think. Nanny then nodded again and the third assistant promptly removed the silver dome.

Sitting on the shiny silver plate was a pair of white silk butler gloves of the highest quality and a gold embossed envelope propped up between them. Charles saw the fine display on the silver tray and his eyes widened.

Nanny fingered the gold envelope and opened it. Then she cleared her throat to be sure that her words would be crisp and clean sounding. "Charles, as a Nanny who has served the Queen of England, and has been trained with the highest of standards in etiquette, I hereby pronounce you an official butler," she said.

Charles's heart skipped a beat or two and he almost dropped the silver tray.

Maria's face warmed under her soulful smile then quietly she walked up the stairs thinking, what a long night, a wonderful and amazing one. Then she went to bed.

Nanny's assistants noticed that Charles was in shock so they held the silver tray for him.

"Charles, this is your first pair of authentic butler gloves, hand stitched from a special shop in England. And this note, dear Charles, written by me with a gold seal of authenticity, should enable you to be hired anywhere on the planet that you wish to work," Nanny said.

Nanny walked right up to Charles and looked into his smiling eyes.

"But, one thing I want you to always remember, dear sir, is that true happiness for you won't be working for the kings and queens and royalty of the world, but will be found in working for a loving and caring family that will be like your own."

Nanny looked as if she were glancing through the ceiling to the sky, smiling and reminiscing. Then she said, "With that said, Charles, do go and work for the highest of royalty in the land and enjoy finding out on your own."

Then with her usual grace, Nanny handed Charles his first pair of official butler gloves. And, with a bow, she handed him his official embossed letter of approval.

About to burst with glowing happiness with the energy of a solar flare, Charles held his composure one more time for Nanny. Holding his gloves and letter with honor he bowed to her. "Thank you Madam," he said.

Charles couldn't hold his composure any longer, he was beside himself. He ran for the front door, flung it open and, losing all control, yelled out to the moon, "Yahoo! I did it, I'm a butler now! After more than five years of trying I'm a butler!" he said.

Closing the door, Charles ran across the room like an elated child, and hugged Nanny and all three assistants. "I love you all!" he said.

Then, spreading open his gold embossed letter of recognition from Nanny, he read it out loud then kissed Nanny on the cheek. "Thank you, thank you, Madam!" Charles said.

Nanny blushed and giggled while saying, "My, oh my."

Nanny and her three assistants laughed and cheered with applause for Charles.

"Charles?"

"Yes, Madam."

"Sometimes, no matter how much etiquette you administer, your madam or sire may not concur. My madam refuses to address me as Nanny. She has always wanted me to refer to her as Maria. But, I won't break my work ethic and call her by her first name. I shall never budge, never. Always hold true to your training, Charles," Nanny said.

Charles straightened up again saying, "Nanny you are the finest in the world. It has been an honor and a privilege to have been your intern. I have truly been blessed. Thank you for preparing my future as a great butler. I won't let you down, Madam."

Before retreating to her quarters Nanny said her goodbyes. "Merry Christmas everyone. Thank you all for your diligence and have a good night."

She stopped and turned with her hand on the door frame

and said, "Dear Charles, do keep in touch, I want a progress report along the way."

Charles with a bow and a smile said, "But of course, Madam."

Everyone went home happy. Nanny looked in her full-length mirror tugging her dress in place and said to herself, "Good luck out there, dear Charles." She then smiled to herself in satisfaction. Nanny had run another superb Christmas Eve party for her humble family in their loving, caring home. She clicked off the antique lamp on her nightstand and started to fall asleep. And then the light clicked back on.

"Tomorrow's Christmas," she said.

Nanny decided to have a moment to herself so she headed out the front door in her pajamas and robe. She turned around in the middle of the dirt road and faced the Vincente home that was still lit up beautifully for Christmas. With her hands in her robe pockets, Nanny took a few steps up the road while looking at the ground, then looked up again at the decorated home flashing Christmas colors in the silence of the night.

"I hope everyone is happy back at home in England. Merry Christmas everyone. I miss you and I love you," Nanny said. Then she looked back up at the beautiful home where she lived and worked for such a loving family, and she felt her smile glow with Christmas warmth.

"Thank you, God, and Merry Christmas," she said.

On the way back in the house Nanny passed by My Pig's pen. "Where are you, My Pig? Please come home," she said.

One more glance at the Christmas lights, one more glance of hope at My Pig's pen, and Nanny walked in the house and closed the tall oak doors behind her. The Vincente home stood glowing in the night. Then in an instant the Christmas lights went out and all was asleep but the crickets that performed in harmony under the stars.

Chapter Twenty-six

Christmas morning was cold but the sun rose in the east with promises.

Anna had already turned the Christmas tree lights on and started a warm fire in the family room. Once she placed the last plate on the breakfast table she began cooking the family Christmas breakfast as she had for the past few years.

Nanny had Christmas day off and as well as New Year's Eve when Maria cooked the family a special dinner.

Anna sang and whistled to Christmas music while she flipped the bacon and stirred the eggs. "Oh my gosh, Frankie is okay and he's safe at home for Christmas, I'm so happy!" she said. She pushed her long black hair back over her shoulder and clapped her hands together one time. All finished, I'll just turn the burners to warm and wake everyone now, she thought.

Her slender feminine hand knocked on Nanny's door first. "Merry Christmas, Nanny, breakfast is ready!" she said.

Then Anna ran up the stairway and stopped about halfway up announcing in joy, "Merry Christmas everyone, breakfast is ready, Merry Christmas!" she said.

"Merry Christmas, Anna! We'll be right down, dear," Maria said.

Nanny listened from her quarters for everyone to be seated first before she too joined the breakfast table.

Anna hugged everyone with joy. "Merry Christmas, Papa! Merry Christmas, Mama!" "Merry Christmas, my good daughter," Antonio said.

"Merry Christmas, honey. What a beautiful breakfast you've created," Maria said.

"Anna dear, if you keep this up I'm afraid I'll lose my position," Nanny said.

"Good, then I could call you Elaine," Maria said.

Everyone laughed at Maria's joke; then silence took over so as not to stir up Maria and Nanny's debate.

Antonio had his hand on his chin in deep thought.

"What are you thinking about, Papa?" Anna said.

"You know, I don't know why I feel this way but I just had a strong feeling flow through me that something powerful is going to take place," Antonio said.

Maria stood up. "Excuse me everyone. I'm going to wake Frankie now. I was letting him sleep to the last minute," she said.

Maria tapped on Frankie's door once, twice, and no answer so she walked in. Looking at the pile of gifts from the party guests piled on Frankie's floor, Maria noticed that only one was opened with the Christmas wrapping thrown about. She looked up and saw Frankie sitting up in his bed wearing his new baseball glove but she didn't notice his quiet tears.

"Merry Christmas, honey!" Maria said.

When Frankie didn't answer, she sat next to him and kissed him on his forehead. Her heart dropped when she saw his sad face. Grabbing a tissue Maria wiped his tears.

"Frankie, honey, it's Christmas morning, your favorite time of year. Anna has made everyone a nice breakfast and we have a fire and the Christmas tree lights are on and Santa Claus came late in the night with lots of gifts. Come on, dear, we are all waiting for you at the table," Maria said.

Frankie got that empty look in his eyes again. His face showed no emotion while he sat there in his bed staring at his new baseball glove on his left hand.

"I love My Pig," he said.

Maria took a tissue, then stood up and walked away, not wanting Frankie to see her tears. "I'll go get your papa," she said. On her solemn walk downstairs Maria saw her family talking with Christmas cheer.

When Antonio saw her face he knew right away what was wrong.

"Come on, Maria, let's go up to his room together," Antonio said.

"Frankie, its Christmas morning. This is no time for sadness, son." Antonio said.

Frankie sniffled, looking up at his Papa with a faint smile through his tears. "God loves me," he said.

"Yes, son, he does."

"Papa?"

"Yes, son?"

"Does he love My Pig?"

Maria looked at Antonio nodding her head up and down and Antonio said, "Yes, Frankie, God loves My Pig."

Frankie stared at the ceiling.

Anna and Nanny were at the breakfast table feeling very concerned for Frankie. "Don't worry about breakfast, Nanny, I have everything on warm; it'll be fine. Let's just pray for Frankie to come out of that bedroom and be well for Christmas," Anna said.

Anna and Nanny finished praying and said, "Amen."

Anna got up and went to the kitchen to pour Nanny and herself some tea. Right about the time the golden brown liquid splashed in the bottom of her tea cup Anna heard screaming coming from somewhere outside. She put the teapot down and looked out the kitchen window.

Then Nanny heard the screaming. "Who in the Queen of England is that screaming?" Nanny said.

The screaming got closer and more persistent.

Anna stood on her tiptoes so she could get a better look at the road. She heard screaming but only saw the empty dirt road and grapevines. The screaming got closer and closer and then Anna saw her. "What the heck? There's a little red-headed girl running up the road screaming," she said.

"What's she saying?" Nanny said.

"Frankie, she's screaming Frankie's name! That must be Katie, that girl that Frankie has spoken about," Anna said.

Katie yelled at the top of her lungs, "Frankie, Frankie!" she said. She dug her feet in the dirt road harder with each stride, running as fast as she could. "Frankie! Frankie!"

Nanny and Anna heard the screams clearly when Katie rounded the empty pig pen for the front porch. Her long red hair flowed behind her in the wind. She never stopped running until her hands slammed on the Vincente's door like drumbeats. Nanny and Anna ran to the front door and Anna swung it open.

Katie put her hands on her bent knees for a moment drawing in deep breaths of air.

"I'm Katie and I've found My Pig!" she said.

Nanny and Anna's faces lit up with surprise.

Katie sucked in more air. "Where's Frankie?!" she said.

Anna pointed up to Frankie's bedroom door. "His room is there, he's right up there in his room!" Anna said.

Katie pushed her way through the taller two ladies and ran up the stairs as fast as she could, skipping every other step and yelling out, "Frankie, Frankie!"

Maria's head turned so fast towards Frankie's door she almost gave herself a whiplash.

Antonio looked up puzzled at the little red-headed girl.

Frankie thought he was dreaming about school when he saw Katie burst into his bedroom yelling his name.

"Frankie, let's go!" Katie said.

Frankie couldn't believe Katie was at the foot of his bed while he was lying there teary-faced in his 49er's football print pajamas.

Katie pointed toward Frankie's door, and yelled, "We have to get to the fairgrounds before Farmer Bob claims a prize for My Pig!" she said.

Katie threw the blankets off Frankie. "Get up now!" she said.

Frankie was stone frozen in disbelief. Katie slapped his shoulder hard. "Get dressed and let's get My Pig before it's too late!" Katie said.

That's all Frankie needed to hear, he flew out of bed to his dresser so fast it was like he didn't even touch one foot on the floor. He got dressed on the run tripping over his baseball glove and without thinking he just picked it up and ran with it under his arm like a football.

Maria froze in place with her hands cupped over her mouth in happy disbelief.

Antonio moved fast, taking charge. "Maria, get dressed now!" he said.

Running over to the stair bannister Antonio looked down at Anna and Nanny and yelled, "Nanny, fire up the old pick-up truck! Anna, hop in back of the truck!" Antonio said.

"Yes sir!" Nanny said.

"Okay, Papa!" Anna said.

"We have to hurry, Nanny! I'm just staying in my Christmas pajamas," Anna said.

Nanny ran for the key rack and threw Anna the old farm

truck keys across the kitchen. "Anna, here's the keys. Go and fire up the truck, I'll just throw on some sweats and sneakers real fast!" Nanny said.

Maria was pacing back in forth in front of her dresser half in shock at the sudden change of events when Antonio came to her rescue.

"Honey, throw this dress on and put on these shoes and let's run, now, honey!" Antonio said.

Once Maria got dressed Antonio grabbed her by the shoulders and shook her gently before kissing her on the mouth. "Maria, everyone is in the truck waiting for us, Merry Christmas honey, we're going to get My Pig!" Antonio said.

When Antonio and Maria got to the pickup truck Nanny had the door opened and the engine running. Anna, Katie, and Frankie were in the back of the truck in the open-air bed.

"Hurry Papa, hurry Mama!" Frankie said.

Maria sat in the middle and Antonio sat shotgun.

"Shouldn't you be driving, Antonio," Maria said.

"Hit it, Nanny!" Antonio said.

Nanny had the old truck in first gear and ready to go when she pressed the throttle all the way down. The riders in the back slid a bit then grabbed on to the sides of the truck.

"Wahoo!" Katie said.

"Hold on!" Anna yelled.

"Maria, don't worry honey, Nanny has taken this old pickup to the grocery store for years. She drives it better than I do," Antonio said.

Maria held on to the metal dash board leaning forward with a big smile. "That's my girl, Elaine!" she said. After shifting into third gear Nanny pointed to herself then to Maria then to herself again saying, "Nanny, Madam, Nanny," she said.

Maria and Antonio broke out in laughter flying down the dirt road for the fair grounds.

When the reality hit Frankie that they were going to get My Pig he got on his knees holding onto the top of the truck cab and yelled at the top of his lungs, "Merry Christmas!"

Everyone at the same time in the truck yelled and Nanny leaned on the horn, "Merry Christmas!" they said.

Frankie noticed a big black raven flying fast in front of them. It was like the raven was heading for the fair too. When the truck sped faster than the bird could fly Frankie looked directly up passing under it. He could have sworn the raven looked right at him with yellow eyes and cawed.

Nanny got a firm grip on the big old steering wheel and hung a hard right. "Hold on!" she said.

Everyone shifted in the truck and there was the fairgrounds hosting the annual San Joaquin Valley Christmas morning county fair. Cars were parked everywhere. Cars were on the sides of the road and filling up the fairground dirt lots. People were walking to the fair from all directions.

There were Christmas decorations everywhere. People were eating red, green, and white popcorn. Kids had big red and white suckers and they were going on rides and playing games. Aromas of food and caramel apples filled the air. Music was coming from the big dirt arena while a couple thousand people sat in the stands cheering on some of California's best prize-winning farm animals.

Katie stood on her feet in the back of the truck and leaned over the side with her face as close to Nanny's window as she could get. "Head for the big arena that way!" she said.

Frankie, Katie, and Anna were all standing up in the back of the truck while Nanny drove into the dirt parking lot.

Frankie's heart was pounding out of his chest like a red

boxing glove about to pop him in the chin, although his head was craned so high looking for My Pig through the crowd that the punch would have probably missed.

Katie's eyes lit up like bright blue spotlights, her finger pointing to the middle of the arena. "Over there, Frankie! Over there! There's My Pig! Let's go!" she said.

When Frankie saw My Pig at the end of a rope leash held by Farmer Bob in the middle of the arena, he about flew right out of his shoes.

Dropping his baseball glove, Frankie flew for the white ranch style fence like a warrior heading in to battle. Nothing and no one would stop Frankie from getting to My Pig.

Frankie and Katie landed on the inside of the fence and together they sprinted across the arena. Katie yelled to Frankie as they ran, "Farmer Bob and My Pig are up next! We have to stop the show!"

In the middle of the arena surrounded by a large stadium full of fans was a lineup of show animals and their masters, led by an announcer with a microphone. The announcer wore a Christmas colored cowboy outfit with a big white cowboy hat and he was beside himself when he saw Frankie and Katie running towards the show animals and their masters during the middle of the biggest show of the year. He started yelling at Frankie and Katie to get out of there.

The audience started getting upset and started throwing Christmas colored popcorn down into the arena and yelling. The cowboy announcer got on his mic and started calling for security over the loud stadium speakers. "Security to the arena, security!" he said.

Frankie ran for My Pig with all he had. "My Pig! My Pig!" Frankie said.

My Pig heard Frankie's voice and he turned and saw

Frankie running for him. My Pig went wild. He started oink-ing and jumping and spinning and shaking his head back and forth like a caught wild animal on the end of Farmer Bob's leash.

Farmer Bob held on with all his might. Then Frankie leaped upon My Pig, wrapping his arms around his entire body like he was hugging someone for dear life. Frankie's face was pressed upon the back of the pig's neck like they were attached with glue. My Pig's head was pointed skyward in a continuous oinking of joy, showing the extreme smile in his eyes.

Katie made it to Farmer Bob and tugged on his worn blue overalls while taking a deep breath trying to catch her wind. Looking up over Farmer Bob's big stomach and big white beard, her young light blue eyes full of adrenalin met his old dark blue eyes full of wonder.

"This is Frankie's pet pig. He belongs to Frankie. He was so sad when My Pig went missing that he had to go to the hospital and he almost died!" Katie said.

The crowd fed off of each other and got louder and louder. Katie tugged and tugged on farmer Bob's overalls. She looked up into Farmer Bob's eyes pleading, "Please help, please sir!" she said.

Farmer Bob looked at Frankie hugging My Pig and then down at Katie pleading for his help and his heart sank. Farmer Bob walked over and spoke to the announcer. "It's okay, sir. This is the boy's pig, not mine. The boy and girl will take over from here," he said.

Farmer Bob walked over to Frankie and patted him on the back. He looked at Katie and winked at her with a big smile and a thumb's up.

Katie returned Farmer Bob's smile. "Thank you, sir!" she said.

Frankie was clasped onto My Pig down in the dirt, oblivious to the commotion around him.

The announcer remembered what he saw on the news. Oh my gosh, this must be the boy that the news was about, wow! he thought. Then he stood at attention, and with the microphone up to his mouth and one hand high in the air he addressed the audience. "It's okay, it's okay! There has been a sudden change of events!" he said. He waved his arms up and down attempting to quiet the frantic audience. Slowly they began to simmer down and start listening. The colorful popcorn cascading from the stands subsided. The security guards stopped at the fence and listened in. The cowboy announcer's voice echoed through the loud speakers out into the grandstands.

"This Pig belongs to this boy! He will continue to show his pet pig," the announcer said.

Katie knew she had to do something. She walked up to the announcer and he looked down at Katie and tilted his white cowboy hat to her. Katie sensed the friendliness in the man's wrinkled face. She reached her hand up to him and he knew exactly what she wanted. Handing her the microphone, the friendly cowboy wished her good luck.

Word spread quickly through the crowd as they began to realize the boy hugging the pig was the boy that the local news story was about. When the crowd saw the little red-headed girl with the microphone they quieted down in wonder and began to listen.

Little Katie stood tall and confident toward the large crowd. Holding the microphone close to her mouth, she began to speak while waving one hand high in the air.

"I'm Katie. They call me Red Headed Kate and this is Frankie Vincente and his best friend who he calls My Pig. You might have heard about them lately on the news!" Katie said.

"That's him! That's the boy that was missing his pig. He's out of the hospital!" a boy in the audience said.

Christmas colored popcorn flew again from the audience's hands. But this time they were throwing it straight up in the sky in celebration, while the audience went wild with cheering and applause.

Chapter Twenty-seven

Frankie was still on his knees in the dirt, hugging, petting and talking to My Pig. Katie walked over and bent down with the microphone under her arm to take the rope leash off of My Pig's neck. The audience could hear My Pig oinking next to the microphone.

The announcer walked around clapping his hands high over his head getting the audience excited.

Katie walked to the middle of the arena holding the rope leash over her head with both arms. She put the leash over her shoulder and said in the microphone, "My Pig doesn't need a leash with Frankie." The crowd went wild. Frankie was now on one bent knee with one arm around My Pig watching Katie.

She walked back to Frankie and held the mic down at her side. "Frankie, when I throw the leash to the ground you go run two laps around the arena with My Pig following you. You got it?" Katie said.

"Yes, Katie, I got it," Frankie said.

"Good, Frankie!"

She put the mic back up to her mouth and her voice sounded throughout the grandstand. "Ladies and Gentlemen! Frankie is going to show you the smartest pig in the world! First, let's get rid of this!" Katie said. When she threw the rope leash across the arena and it landed on the ground, Frankie took off running. After Frankie got about fifteen yards away My Pig took off running after him and the crowd went wild with applause. During the entire two laps they yelled, hooted, and stomped their feet.

Katie yelled into the mic again. "Now Frankie is going to demonstrate how My Pig can count the fish that Frankie catches!" Katie said.

Some of the audience started mumbling amongst each other while others clapped and cheered.

Katie lowered the mic again. "Frankie, you can do it, get over here next to me. All you have to do is pretend you and My Pig are fishing at the pond."

"Okay, I can do that," Frankie said.

When the noise of the crowd lowered to faint chatter, Katie raised the mic back to her mouth and started to speak before she was rudely interrupted by a man wearing a trucker cap with a deep loud voice that echoed through the arena.

"That pig can't count no fish, get it out of here!" he said.

Chatter and laughter and debating engulfed the crowd.

Frankie heard the rude man criticize My Pig and he didn't like it at all. Frankie glared up at the loud rude man and puffed his chest a little while raising his chin and clenching his fists. Then Frankie turned his head towards Katie. She had never seen Frankie with that strength.

"What do you want me to do, Katie?" Frankie said.

Katie's head went back and she put her hand to her chest in surprise. "Wait right here!" she said. Katie looked funny scurrying all around the dirt arena and staring at the ground and her red hair bouncing with every step. Some of the audience laughed. Others started getting impatient until they saw Katie run back to Frankie holding three sticks, each about the size of a fish.

She leaned closer to Frankie and spoke to him. "Just start out with your fishing wish and then toss out your imaginary fishing line and catch a fish. Pretend you're at the pond with

My Pig. I'll guide you, Frankie. Are you ready?"

"Yes, Katie, I'm ready," Frankie said.

Katie held the mic to Frankie's mouth so he could be heard through the loudspeakers across the grandstands. "Frankie, start with your fishing wish," Katie said. The audience was eager to see what was going to happen next.

Frankie began singing with passion, "Gonna catch a trout, I have no doubt, or maybe it's a bass I pull out of class, cat fish, cat fish, put you on my dish!"

Women and girls whistled and cheered throughout the audience in approval of Frankie's voice.

A girl stood up and yelled across the arena, "Frankie, you're cute!"

Girls clapped and hollered at Frankie. Men and children cheered Frankie on.

Frankie flung his imaginary fishing rod forward, tossing an imaginary hook and worm across the arena.

He waited a few seconds then yelled into the mic, "I got one!"

My Pig felt Frankie's energy and recognized his words. He stood up on all fours feeling excited.

"Here it comes, My Pig, get ready!" Frankie said.

With perfect timing Frankie whipped the fish out of the imaginary pond as Katie threw the stick on the bank.

"One fish caught!" Frankie said.

My Pig, right on cue, jumped up once and oinked. People in the audience nodded their heads up and down and clapped lightly at the first fish. A small group of young women whistled and cheered.

Katie turned the mic to her lips, then back to Frankie's. "Now My Pig will count two fish," she said.

The audience watched on. Frankie cast out again and

hooked up.

"One quick yank to set the hook and another to bring the fish in," he said.

Frankie's back was bent and his hands kept busy reeling his imaginary rod and reel. Katie threw the second stick-fish onto the imaginary bank of the imaginary pond. My Pig stood up on all fours oinking. Then, he jumped up and down with his front legs twice.

The announcer lifted his white cowboy hat to the audience and they clapped and stomped their feet a little harder this time.

Katie turned the mic to her lips and spoke in it, "Now, ladies and gentlemen, you are about to witness My Pig count out three fish by jumping up and down three times! You will never see this anywhere else but right here right now!"

The rude man stood up, cupping his hands to his mouth saying, "That pig can't do it, I tell you! It won't be able to count three fish!"

Katie stomped a foot on the ground, sending up dust. Her lips were puckered and she glared up at the grandstands where she heard the man's voice.

Katie grasped the mic and stepped away from Frankie for a moment and said, "You're going to lose your shirt on this one, Mister!"

The crowd mocked the rude man and they threw popcorn and stomped their feet on the bleachers causing a rumble through the fairgrounds. The loud applauding attracted people from all over the fairgrounds. The Walnut Street School baseball team was showing up all decked out in their baseball uniforms.

"What is all that excitement at the arena?" Calvin said.

"L-Let's go see," Billy said.

Chad took off his ball cap and started walking to the arena fence to get a look. Calvin, Billy, and other team members followed. They all gathered on the white fence right next to the Vincente's.

Chad whispered to Calvin, "That's Rich Boy's family," he said. Calvin didn't even look up at the Vincente's. Billy stood high up on the fence examining the action in the arena.

"That's Fr-Frankie! He has My P-Pig!" Billy said.

Billy was so relieved to see the pig and Frankie that he almost ran into the arena and tackled them.

"Yes! They found him!" Chad said.

Calvin blew out a sigh of relief. I'm not going to jail for murder, he thought.

Antonio was standing at the fence next to Maria with Anna and Nanny. Heavy chatter, car doors slamming, and people scattering from behind got Anna's attention.

"The news crew is here, Papa," Anna said.

Mary Winthorp and a cameraman nudged their way through the baseball players and small crowd at the arena fence. Another crewman followed.

"Clear the way, we're going live!" Mary Winthorp said. She quickly fixed her hair, looking in a small mirror, straightened her blouse, and cleared her throat.

"Roll 'um!" a crewman said.

The Vincente's scooted together in a little huddle to give the news crew enough room. Anna yelled so the baseball team could hear her, "Hey Mama and Papa, Frankie's going to be on the news! My brother is a star!" she said.

All attention was on Frankie and My Pig.

Katie stood and nodded at Frankie. After checking on his pig, Frankie nodded back confirming he was ready.

Katie addressed the waiting crowd through the microphone

saying, "Ladies and gentlemen! You are about to witness the smartest pig in the world. My Pig will now count Frankie's third caught fish!" Katie said.

Katie ran over and whispered in Frankie's ear, "Make them wait longer this time," she said. Then she held the microphone for him.

This time Frankie went through the whole motion of fishing at the pond. He first tied a new imaginary hook on his line. Then opened up a can of worms and pulled out a long wiggly worm. "Okay, Mr. Wiggler, time for you to take a dunk," he said. He put the imaginary worm on his imaginary hook, then cast out. "Ker plunk," Frankie said.

Giggles and ah's flowed through the crowd.

Frankie tugged a couple times on his imaginary rod. My Pig sat at attention and oinked a couple times. Katie kept on holding the microphone up to Frankie while the crowd looked on.

"Look at all the dragonfly's on the pond today, My Pig," Frankie said.

"Oink, oink!" My Pig said.

Frankie became a showman and put the audience on the edge of their seats. "Cat fish, cat fish, put you on my dish. Got one!" he said.

He pulled up on the rod and started reeling in. The crowd watched with intent. Frankie arched his back, pulling in the large fish. Reeling, reeling, and pulling.

The Vincente's and the three bullies and the ball team watched from the white fence.

Anna cupped her hands to her mouth and yelled, "You can do it, Frankie!"

Maria's hands were over her mouth, not believing what she was seeing.

The news cameras were rolling.

Frankie grunted into the microphone while Katie did her best to follow his bobbing head with the mic.

"It's a big one! Here it comes, My Pig. Get ready, here it comes!" Frankie said.

With all his might, Frankie pulled the fish out of the water with one big yank on his fishing rod and he swung it around towards My Pig.

With perfect timing Katie tossed the largest stick-fish on the bank of the imaginary pond.

That time My Pig just stood there staring at the stick. He was a little confused that they weren't at the pond.

The crowd watched in silence. The rude doubtful man in the grandstands stood up and was about to take a bow, when Frankie spoke into the microphone as he bent down over My Pig and said, "It's a catfish!"

My Pig jerked with excitement then looked straight up at the sky as a black raven flew overhead, cawing. My Pig squealed loudly at the raven, then he nudged the stick-fish with his pig nose and oinked before jumping up once, twice, then three times with more energy and higher than he ever had before.

Frankie threw the microphone to Katie then fell to his knees, wrapping both arms around My Pig.

"You did it, Frankie! You did it, My Pig!" Katie said.

The crowd rose to their feet and rewarded Frankie and My Pig and Katie with a standing ovation. Christmas popcorn rained into the arena.

Katie yelled into the mic, "Merry Christmas! Yahoo, yes, yes!"

The Christmas cowboy announcer threw his white cowboy hat in the air and started running circles around the arena while raising his arms up high getting the audience going even more.

The Vincente's hugged and danced with joy. The baseball team started running for Frankie and cheering as they hooted and hollered. All except for Calvin. He just sat on the fence looking down at the ground.

Katie jumped up in the air, her red hair flying and her face lit up like the sunshine. She ran over to the announcer and handed him the microphone as the crowd stood cheering. Katie hugged the Christmas cowboy announcer and then ran over to Frankie and My Pig and hugged them both, causing the crowd to cheer louder. Even the rude man was on his feet applauding for My Pig. Baseball players from Frankie's school were in the arena circling Frankie and My Pig cheering them on.

The announcer raised his hat in the air and spoke into the microphone. "Ladies and Gentleman, we have a unanimous decision," He said.

He walked over and grabbed Frankie by the arm, raising it up like a winning prizefighter.

"We have a champion of this year's farm animal competition. Our winner with the largest ovation in this arena's history goes to, Frankie Vincente and My Pig!" the announcer said.

The crowd went wild! Frankie just ran back to hug his little pig. My Pig oinked and jumped around with excitement. Katie stood near Frankie and My Pig, joining the audience in the standing ovation.

A man walked across the arena holding a trophy in one hand. The trophy was a beautiful mixture of oak, walnut, and cherry woods, hand carved into a Santa Claus surrounded by a few farm animals and topped with a gold plated Christmas tree.

At the base of the trophy was a gold plaque that said "San Joaquin Christmas Fair

Champion, Best Farm Animal." In the man's other hand was a billboard-size check for $1,000.

Katie patted Frankie on the back, trying to get his attention away from My Pig for a moment. "Stand up and collect your prize!" she said.

Frankie stood and the man handed him his trophy in front of the applauding audience. "Thank you, sir!" Frankie said.

Before giving Frankie his oversized check the man held it up to the audience then left the arena to thunderous applause.

Chapter Twenty-eight

The Vincente's were filled with joy. They had been watching everything from the white fence.

"Come on, honey, let's let him have his moment. Let's go wait in the truck for him," Antonio said. With his arm around his happy wife, Antonio, Maria, Nanny, and Anna walked back to the old farm truck.

The Walnut Street baseball team was surrounding Frankie, Katie, and My Pig with high fives to Frankie and pets and pats for My Pig. Katie was so happy to see the baseball team finally being nice to Frankie. Except for one thing: no Calvin. She looked all around, then saw him sitting alone on the white fence. She saw that the Vincente's were back in the truck and Anna was standing up in the back of the bed keeping her eye on Frankie. The audience was starting to filter out of the grandstands.

Katie sprinted across the arena, stopping right in front of Calvin. She crossed her arms and stomped her foot shooting up a small cloud of dust. Then she leaned forward and looked Calvin right in the eyes. "Don't you think you've done enough harm, enough bullying? He could have died in that hospital. Calvin, it's only right that you walk up there to Frankie and invite him to play in the big game today!" Katie said.

Calvin sat on that white ranch fence staring down at his cleats and adjusting his laces. He rubbed his chin in thought. Out of nowhere a raven dive-bombed Calvin as if to peck him on the head. Calvin ducked and looked up wide-eyed at the sky but nothing was there.

When the shocking current of fear wore off, Calvin thought, where did that bird come from? It had yellow eyes that looked right through me. Strange, ravens don't have yellow eyes, he thought.

"Yeah, I guess you're right, Katie," Calvin said.

Katie stomped her foot and pointed to Frankie and the rest of the players that were surrounding Frankie and My Pig. "Go out there and talk to him, Calvin," she said.

Calvin walked with Katie towards Frankie across the dirt arena. The audience was emptying out and the team was heading for the baseball field. Frankie was surprised to see Calvin approaching him.

I won't let him touch me or My Pig, Frankie thought. He doubled his fist this time, getting ready for Calvin.

"It's okay, Frankie," Katie said. Then she crossed her arms and glared at Calvin.

"Rich Boy, where's your uniform? How you gonna play in the big game without your uniform?" Calvin said.

"Huh, what do you mean?" Frankie said.

Calvin took the team cap off his head and said, "Here you go, Rich Boy, this will get you through the game." Then he put the cap on Frankie's head and lightly tapped the brim down. "We need a left fielder. The game's about to start."

When Calvin turned to walk away Katie jumped up and down with joy. "Yaaay! You're playing in the big game today, Frankie, just like you always wanted!" Katie said.

She was so happy for Frankie that she hugged him and gave him a kiss on the cheek. "Merry Christmas, Frankie!" Katie said.

Frankie looked at his trophy and award check and watched Calvin walking away. "Calvin, stop!" Frankie said. My Pig hid behind Frankie and observed Calvin from between Frankie's legs.

"Yeah, what is it, Rich Boy?" Calvin said.

Frankie set his trophy on the ground and jogged over to Calvin. "I won this and, uh, I'm giving it to you, Calvin and you, Katie. You will get five hundred dollars each." Then he handed Calvin the real $1,000 check without even thinking twice about it. Frankie took a deep breath and, looking down at the ground, he said, "Merry Christmas, Calvin."

Katie hugged Frankie again, saying, "Wow! Five hundred dollars. Thank you, Frankie!"

Calvin stood there mesmerized staring at the largest check he had ever seen in his life.

Frankie and Katie headed for the old truck with My Pig following right on Frankie's heels.

Antonio was honking the horn. Maria and Nanny's big smiles shined through the window and Anna was standing up in back of the truck waving and yelling, "Congratulations, Frankie, congratulations!"

Katie took Frankie's trophy from him. "You've got to get to the baseball field, go and get your glove," she said.

Frankie looked into Katie's eyes for a moment, then like lightning he bolted for the truck.

Antonio got out and greeted his victorious son. He enveloped Frankie in a big bear hug, congratulating him.

"Papa, we can't go home yet. We have to get to the baseball field on the double. I'm playing in the big game!" Frankie said.

"That's my boy!" Antonio said.

Katie and Anna struggled with my pig in their arms and finally got him in the back of the truck.

"Hop in, let's roll!" Antonio said.

Frankie was so excited that he leaped in the back of the old truck landing on his back laughing. My Pig attacked him with oinks.

"I'm playing in the big game, yahoo!" Frankie said.

"Next stop the baseball field!" Antonio said.

Maria and Nanny were embracing each other's arms in and exchange of smiles.

Anna had an ear-to-ear smile. "I'm so happy, Frankie has dreamed of playing in this game for so long," she said.

Chapter Twenty-nine

Calvin stood in the middle of the empty arena staring at the check Frankie had given him. He was feeling confused. Something was happening deep within Calvin that he didn't understand. He was in a time warp, not thinking or knowing how long he had been standing there. Finally, Calvin realized God had just spoken to him. He was amazed and in a pleasant state of shock.

Antonio parked the truck at the baseball field. "You ladies go and grab some good seats and I'll be there in a while," he said. "Come on, son, I'll walk you over to the diamond.

Father and son stood in silence in awe of the magnificent baseball stadium. Plush dark green grass, perfectly drawn white chalk lines connecting brand new bright white bases. A new electronic scoreboard that looked just like the one that the pros used stood tall. Professional style dugouts for each team had been added. And most of all the baseball field had renovated stadium-style seating that sat five thousand people who came from all over.

Fried foods and the aroma of fresh baked candies and pies filled the air. Food servers were selling Christmas colored popcorn, candy apples and hot apple cider up and down the stands. You could smell the caramel on the apples and the cinnamon warming in the cider. Sweet aromas blended in the air teasing people as they raised their hands for some. Hand held inflatable Santa's and reindeers attached to sticks bobbed up and down over fairgoers heads. Girls and boys were shooting free prizes from huge sling shots out to the audience. People were dressed in Christmas colors and many had Christmas pajamas on.

"I like your hat, son," Antonio said.

"Thank you, Papa," Frankie said.

"Do you know, Frankie, what the most important thing about this game is?"

"What's that, Papa?"

"It's that you just have fun, son. That's all, just go out there and have as much darn fun playing this great American game as you can. It doesn't matter if you win or lose. Just have a grape-pickin' blast, just enjoy every second of it, son. Can you do that for me?" Antonio said.

"Yes, you're right, Papa, I'm going to just have a ton of fun," Frankie said.

"That's my boy. I'll be watching you with your mama, sister, Nanny, and Katie. Go get 'em son, I love you!" Antonio said.

"Bye, Papa!" Frankie said. I guess I'll just head for the dugout, Frankie thought.

"H-hey what are you d-doing here, Fr-Frankie?" Billy said.

"Calvin gave me his hat and said for me to play left field," Frankie said.

"I'll t-tell T-Ted f-for you," Billy said.

"Hello, Frankie. My name is Ted. I'm the assistant captain behind Calvin. Billy told me all about it, welcome to the team," Ted said. "That sure was a great show you and that pig put on today."

"Hey everyone, listen up! Frankie is playing left field today. Let's give him a welcoming round of applause!" Ted announced.

The team clapped loudly and whistled for Frankie.

"Our left fielder hurt his hand last night at practice. Can

you catch high flies?" Ted said.

"Uh, I think so," Frankie said.

"Go ahead and get out in left field, Frankie, and let's see what you got," Ted said.

"He's running to the wrong field!" a player said.

"Hey, your other left!" Ted said.

When Frankie turned to go to left field he tripped over his own feet. The team laughed at Frankie. He got out there and bent his knees a little and slammed his fist into his new glove.

Antonio got to his seat. "Great job, girls. You got us seats right behind home plate!" Antonio said.

"Sit down, honey. I've been waiting for you," Maria said.

"That's some nice looking cotton candy you have, Anna and Katie," Antonio said.

"Here, Nanny, want a bite?" Anna said.

"It's too early for sweets, thank you," Nanny said.

"Oh, Nanny, it's Christmas. Loosen up a little. After all, you're wearing your old pair of sweats in public," Anna Said.

Anna and Katie busted up laughing at Nanny.

Nanny looked at Anna up and down and laughed. "Oh, I guess you're right with code, Miss Pajamas in public," Nanny said. Then she slumped in her chair a little, finally relaxing. "To heck with etiquette at the ball game, give me a caramel apple and a warm cinnamon cider!" Nanny said.

Anna and Katie clapped and laughed for Nanny. "That's it Nanny!" Anna said.

"Papa, look, the game is starting and Frankie is out in left field!" Anna said.

"No, not yet, Anna, they're just practicing. But you're right, look at our boy out there!" Antonio said.

"Look, Elaine, that's our boy!" Maria said.

Nanny leaned over holding her candy apple and cider

in her old sweats toward Maria and said, "It's Nanny! Call me Nanny. I was trained at the finest school of etiquette at Cambridge London, Madam." Then, cupping her hands around her mouth the best she could while grasping her goodies Nanny turned her attention back to the ballgame and yelled out in a thick British accent, "Go lad, go Frankie!"

Maria looked up in the sky with a big smile. "Thank you, Lord, for healing our son in so many ways," she said.

Ted picked up a bat and ball and walked over to home plate. "Well, he made it to the correct field so far," he said.

The team laughed again. The crowd was starting to fill the stands. Frankie saw them lining up and walking to their seats. He pushed his hat up on his head a little, took a big breath, and tried to relax his shoulders, then refocused on home plate.

Ted rested the baseball bat over his right shoulder and threw the ball up and down a couple times in his left hand. Then he threw the ball up in the air and swung the bat sending the ball very high into center field.

"Wow, Great hit!" a player said.

"He'll never catch it," another player said.

Anna watched the ball flying high in the sky. "Uh oh, that's way up there," she said.

"You can do it, son," Antonio said.

"Oh dear," Nanny said.

Katie was crossing her fingers on both hands while she looked in the sky at the baseball.

Maria watched in silence with her hand on top of her head.

I was just at the hospital with him, and now I'm watching a baseball coming down at him like a bomb, Maria thought.

Frankie watched the high flying ball, judging its height and distance. While his head was aimed to the sky he quickly threw off Calvin's hat and took off in a full sprint toward center field. Adjusting to the ball he ran out farther toward the wall.

Katie watched with much hope. "Catch it, Frankie!" Katie yelled.

Keeping his eye on the ball, Frankie took his last long stride and leaped into the air. His body was stretched out as far as possible, his arm extended, his glove reaching. The baseball made a thumping sound. With his glove squeezed shut Frankie landed on the grass hard smashing into the earth with a deep "oof." With his eyes closed Frankie slid across the grass receiving a burning green stain on his forearm before coming to a halt.

Frankie lay planted between left and center field. He was on his side with his gloved arm fully extended in front of him. His right arm was bent back behind him. He spat a couple times to get the grassy dirt out of his mouth. No one knew, including Frankie, if he was lying on the ball or if it was in his glove.

Do I have it? Frankie thought.

Without moving he took a deep breath. Lying there with all eyes on him, Frankie's head dropped as if his neck wore out. He raised an open glove towards the team and audience. The white of the baseball stood out inside the glove's tanned leather.

They're clapping, I must have the ball! Frankie thought.

He turned his glove towards himself and saw the ball. "I caught it!" Frankie said. He lay there displaying his prize with a smile from ear to ear.

The Vincentes, Nanny, and Katie were on their feet yelling with joy.

"That's my boy! Merry Christmas to all!" Antonio said.

Like a chain reaction people in the audience started yelling out, "Merry Christmas!" You could hear the crowd yelling throughout the fair grounds.

Maria acted like a little girl slapping Antonio on the shoulder, "Look what you started," she said.

"Give me a high five, Papa!" Anna said.

Frankie smiled and raised a hand to the audience, brushing the grass off his pants and shirt. The game starts in about twenty minutes, he thought.

Ted ran out to the pitcher's mound clapping and yelling to Frankie, "Amazing catch Frankie, amazing, welcome to the Walnut Street Ravens!"

The rest of the team ran onto the field to warm up.

The Walnut Street Ravens wore maroon jerseys with big black birds on the back with spread wings. Over the top of the raven it said "Walnut Street" and under the bird it said "Ravens." Their caps had a light gray crown with a raven on front and maroon brims. Their baseball pants were gray and maroon pinstripes and they wore maroon baseball socks.

They had ten minutes to throw the ball around. Then the visiting team, the Sacramento Eagles, which were the Northern California State Champions, would get the field for their warm-ups. The Eagles wore blue and white uniforms with a big eagle on their backs.

Ted, the assistant team captain was becoming concerned. Where's Calvin? He needs to warm up his pitching arm. "Hey, Chad, where's Calvin?" Ted said.

Chad tilted his head and raised his arms, "I don't know, last time I saw him was at the arena."

"Billy, have you seen Calvin?" Ted said.

"Ask Fr-Fr-Frankie," Billy said.

Chad pointed to the parking lot, "I see him, here he comes now!"

Calvin was oblivious to Ted, waving for him from the pitcher's mound. He was still mesmerized by the check in his hand and whatever it was that happened to him when his heart pounded and he heard a powerful voice. He stopped alongside of the old pickup truck and put the check in his pocket and buttoned it. My Pig hunkered down and shook in fear. Calvin stuck his hand in the back of the truck, patting the pig on top of his head and said, "Good fish counting, good pig."

"Wow, look at that big crowd! Man, they made the stadium nice this year," he said. Nodding his head and smiling, he headed for the field. "Let's go win a baseball game, My Pig!"

Chapter Thirty

After the national anthem played with the huge American flag blowing in the breeze the patriotic crowd sat down. The burly umpire bent over home plate, dusting it off with his brush then, standing up with his arms in the air, he said, "Merry Christmas! Play ball!"

The Sacramento Eagle's pitcher stood on the pitcher's mound. He nodded to the catcher and threw the first pitch of the game. Calvin saw the ball coming fast right down the middle but he didn't swing.

"Strike!" the umpire said.

Ted was the first-base coach. He leaned over, yelling out to Calvin, "Wake up, Calvin!"

Another pitch and still Calvin didn't swing. "Strike two!" the umpire said.

The fans of the Sacramento Eagles applauded. Calvin stepped out of the batter's box. The umpire held a hand up to the pitcher, "Hold up!" he said.

Calvin shook his head a couple times, looking out at left field. This is the big game; what am I thinking? I have to win the first trophy for Walnut Street School, Calvin thought.

He stepped up to the plate tapping his bat on his cleats and adjusting his hat. He glared at the pitcher while taking two practice swings.

The Eagles started yelling, "Hey batter, hey batter, batter."

The pitcher chose his pitch and let it fly. Calvin eyed the ball all the way in, connecting a line drive right over third base.

"Yes, Calvin, go to second!" Ted said.

The ball rolled deeply into left field. Calvin held up at second base.

The Ravens were on their feet cheering, "Way to go, Calvin! Wahoo! Nice hit, Calvin!"

Chad stepped up to the plate holding his bat up high and moving it in little circles. Then he squatted low. The pitcher took a second to concentrate as he had a hard time figuring out Chad's stance.

The pitcher didn't realize Chad's favorite pitch was a curve ball and Chad hit the ball high into right center field. The center fielder and the right fielder both ran for the high fly with their gloves outstretched. They jumped for the falling ball and collided into each other with force. As the players lay on the grass the ball spun for a second before coming to a stop.

Calvin tagged up and left for third base and Chad ran for second.

When they realized the outfielders weren't on their feet yet, they kept running. Chad stopped on third base and Calvin headed for home plate. The left fielder ran to assist his fallen teammates. He picked up the ball and sent it to the catcher like a guided missile. Calvin ran for home preparing to go low into a powerful slide.

The catcher, squatting down, blocked home plate with his glove extended. Calvin gritted his teeth and slid into the pitcher. The collision was too much, the catcher dropped the ball.

Frankie was in seventh heaven in the dugout taking in every moment of the game. "Wahoo! We're beating the Eagles one to nothing!"

Excitedly, he took a deep breath. "Okay, okay, just have

fun, a ton of fun," Frankie said to himself.

The Raven's dugout was celebrating their first score. The locals in the crowd cheered on.

"Go, Frankie's team, go Ravens!" Anna and Nanny said.

"You got it, Frankie!" Katie said.

Maria looked lovingly at Antonio clapping for Frankie's team. "Oh, honey, I will never forget this Christmas," she said.

Just have fun Frankie, don't get nervous, Antonio thought.

The next few players batting for the Ravens got out and Chad never made it to third base.

Frankie headed for left field.

"There goes Frankie, Mama!" Anna said.

"That's my boy!" Maria said.

Frankie looked around the stadium. Oh my gosh, I'm really here, I'm in the game, Frankie thought.

The Sacramento Eagles proved to be a challenge for the Walnut Street Ravens. The game progressed to the top of the ninth inning and the Ravens were losing eight to five. Frankie saw Calvin getting more and more stressed out. Everyone's giving up. We've done a good job, and it's not over yet, he thought.

Calvin was getting angry. "You guys can't lose this game for me!" he said. "I'm a star pitcher, damn it!"

Frankie stood up in front of the dugout and spoke. "We're last at bat, it's not over yet."

"What in the heck are you thinking, rich boy!" Calvin said.

"Calvin, let him speak," Ted said.

"L-let him sp-speak, "Billy said.

Calvin gave in and sat down. "You too, Billy! Oh man, now I've seen everything," Calvin said.

"Here, Calvin. You haven't worn your hat all day, put this

back on for the last inning," Frankie said.

"You know I've been watching you guys and you're not having any fun. My papa told me to just go out there and have fun, it doesn't matter if you win or lose. Papa said to just go out there and have a heck of a blast," Frankie said.

"He's right! We haven't been having fun like we usually do," Chad said.

"Heck, Calvin, you haven't teased Billy all day about his stuttering, and I usually tell you that your shoe's untied or your zippers down before you throw your first pitch. We usually make fun of each other and roast the heck out of the other team. Frankie's right, we need to go out there in this last round and just have a good time!" Chad said.

The team started loosening up and making jokes and hitting each other with their ball caps.

The umpire looked at the Raven's dugout. "Batter up, let's go!" he said.

Calvin stood up one more time in front of the dugout before he went up to bat.

"Frankie's right. Okay, dingdongs, let's do it!" Calvin said.

Raising his arms in the air with a smile, Chad said, "Wahoo!"

"You better get up here and play ball!" the umpire said.

"Coming right now, I'm ready, ump," Calvin said.

"Hey, Frankie, you want to start the fun?" Chad said.

"How do you mean?" Frankie said.

"Don't be scared or anything, you'll be like one of the boys. Yell out to Calvin that his zippers down. He probably won't even know who said it anyway. He's busy staring down the pitcher," Chad said.

"Oh, I don't think I should," Frankie said.

"It's okay, really, go ahead, dude," Chad said.

Frankie raised his hand to his mouth and craned his neck from the bench, "Calvin, your zippers down!" Frankie said.

"These pants don't have zippers, you fool!" Calvin said.

"See? He loved it," Chad said.

"Take this one on your beaks, Eagles!" Calvin said.

He swung the bat with all he had and the ball flew into right field.

"Run, dude, run!" Chad said.

"Nice double hit," Frankie said. "Are we having fun yet?"

"Yes! Heck yeah! Wahoo! We're having fun now, Frankie!" some of the team said.

Chad was up at bat next. After two strikes and two balls he got a base hit. Calvin stood on second base and Chad on first base with no outs.

"Nice single, dingle head!" Calvin said.

"You got two more bases to get to home plate, dummy!" Chad said.

"Come on Billy baby. Hit the ball over the fence!" Ted said.

Frankie was happy to see everyone finally having fun. He could hardly wait to get up to bat and have some fun, too— until it was his turn. "Oh, no, I'm up at bat after two outs?" Frankie said.

The team became quiet for a moment so Ted stepped in to give them a pep talk. "Come on guys, what's wrong?" he said. "What happened to just having fun? I know, I know, two outs, bases loaded, top of the ninth, and we are losing by three runs. And, here we are at the annual fairgrounds Christmas game that Walnut Street has never won."

Ted looked up and down the dugout at each player. "If we get one more out, it's all over. To top it off we have a rookie named Frankie up next at bat and he's never even played with us until today. Look around, look at that crowd starting off their Christmas morning with us and having a great time. Look at Calvin, Chad, and Billy on those bases roasting each other. Frankie's played a heck of a game. I know he's struck out a couple times and only got a base hit, but he did get a nice double. We owe him something. We owe him some encouragement," Ted said.

Morey stood up and spoke. Morey was an African American star player and straight-A student. Everyone figured Morey would go pro someday.

"Ted's right!" Morey said. "Let's all stand up and root Frankie on instead of sitting here with our heads up our butts."

Frankie smiled and pointed to the bat section, saying, "I'll take that old wooden bat right there."

"This old thing? Here you go, Frankie," Ted said.

Frankie walked up to home plate mumbling to himself, "Just have fun, grape-pickin fun, a ton of fun."

The local crowd was on their feet. The Ravens yelled and cheered Frankie on. Amongst all the cheering, Frankie heard Morey yelling, "Just have fun, Frankie!" Morey said.

The fans from the bay area started yelling and stomping their feet on the bleachers. The Vincente's were going wild. Katie knew that Frankie wouldn't like all the pressure. "You can do it, Frankie!" she said. Oh no, I need to do something fast, Katie thought.

The pitcher threw a fast ball right down the middle of home plate.

"Strike one!" the umpire said.

Katie ran up to the backstop fence. "Frankie! I'm over here," she said.

Frankie heard her and turned, "Hi, Katie!"

"Frankie, hit a home run for me," Katie said.

"Ok, I'll try."

Katie waved her hand towards the plate, "Go on, do it for me, Frankie."

The Eagles' pitcher had the composure of a pro. He shook his head saying no, but he grinned at the catcher's next signal.

Frankie watched the very crafty curve ball come in.

"Strike two!" the umpire said.

Katie took a big inhale and sprinted for the truck. When she got to the truck she yelled out, "Come with me, My Pig!" She wrestled with the tailgate and could hardly lift My Pig out of the truck. Kneeling down next to the little pig, Katie looked in his eyes and said, "Frankie's over there!"

My Pig saw Frankie standing at home plate with a baseball bat and tore off like a charging bull. My Pig rounded the fence and went on the field running down the first base line for Frankie at home plate.

The umpire lifted off his mask with a look of wonder. "What is going on here? Hold the game!" he said.

When Frankie saw My Pig, he dropped his bat and went to the ground with open arms.

"Hey get that stupid pig out of here!" the pitcher said.

Katie arrived out of breath. "Frankie, I'll hold him behind the backstop so he can see you."

"I love you, My Pig!" Frankie said.

"Play ball!" the umpire said.

The Eagles' outfielders were laughing at Frankie. The left fielder took off his hat and yelled at Frankie, "I'll have your pig for bacon, farm boy!" he said.

Frankie took a few steps toward him and said, "No, I'll have you for bacon!"

"Hey farmer boy, hey batter, batter, hey farmer boy!" the Eagles' team chanted.

Frankie looked the pitcher dead in the eye, his nostrils flaring and his heart pumping harder and harder. He could almost smell bacon cooking when he glared at the left fielder. He glanced over at My Pig behind the backstop with Katie, and then he focused on the pitcher.

The pitch flew for home plate with precision. Frankie eyeballed the baseball and lifting his front foot he cocked his bat and yelled out, "I love My Pig!"

The bat connected with the ball with such velocity that the ball was almost lost in the sky. The ball was soaring, the crowd on their feet, heads lifting, and Frankie's family was clapping loudly with their mouths wide open. Frankie tuned out any sound and, like a slow motion dream, he watched the left fielder run for the back of the fence.

Like a light switch the sound came back on in Frankie's mind and the Walnut Street Ravens were running towards him yelling, "Grand slam home run!"

"We win, we win, yes, Frankie, we win!" they said.

"Lift him up guys. Let's carry him around the bases!" Calvin said.

Antonio ran onto the field and followed the players all the way around the bases with Katie and My Pig right behind him.

"Yahoo, Frankie's a star!" Anna said.

The three ladies jumped up and down hugging each other in a circle of smiles.

"That's my boy, that's my boy!" Maria said.

Nanny raised her hands yelling out to the sky, "Merry Christmas!"

Frankie, on top of his team's shoulders, smiled from ear to ear as he was carried around the bases. The team sang, "Frankie, Frankie, he's the man, he won the game with a big grand slam!"

When Frankie's team set him down on home plate they went wild in celebration. They tackled him and piled on top of him yelling, "Frankie! Frankie, you did it! Yahoo! We won, we won!"

After a long celebration everyone started funneling out of the ballpark.

When things simmered down, Calvin walked up to Frankie. "Frankie, I did pitch a good game today, but we wouldn't have won without your grand slam at the end. Here, dude, take your game-winning hat, you deserved it, and don't worry, I have my jersey for a souvenir. You made my dream come true of being the first pitcher to win the trophy for Walnut Street School," Calvin said.

Putting his hand out, Calvin said, "Uh, and I'm sorry for bullying you all those times, Frankie."

Frankie, looking at the ground, shook Calvin's hand. Then, looking up he said, "Thank you, Calvin, you made my dream come true by letting me play in the game today. Uh, I accept your apology," Frankie said.

Frankie walked toward the truck to his waiting family, and Katie and My Pig. He jumped in back of the truck surrounded by hugs, hooting high fives and oinks of joy when he heard a voice calling to him. It was Billy, who was running for the truck. "Fr-Frankie w-wait a m-minute!" Billy said.

"Papa, stop the truck!" Frankie said.

"Fr-Frankie c-can I g-go f-fishing with you some-some-time?" Billy said.

"Mama, can I take Billy fishing for a little before we open gifts?" Frankie said.

Maria looked back at Billy, sizing him up "Okay, for one hour tops," Maria said.

"Hop in, Billy!" Frankie said.

Nanny drove the old pickup truck for home. She and Maria were chatting away in the front seat with Antonio. Antonio was looking straight ahead up the road thinking about Frankie's grand slam home run.

Frankie, Katie, My Pig, Anna, and Billy were in the back of the truck laughing and carrying on.

In what seemed like a coincidence, Frankie looked to the sky and high above him was that raven. The raven looked right into Frankie's eyes with its wild, expressive yellow eyes and cawed at Frankie as if it were saying goodbye.

Frankie felt a sensation of wonder when he saw the raven turn into a majestic eagle. He watched the eagle swoop down out of the sky in front of the truck and disappear in midair.

I thought there was something about you, raven, Frankie thought. He pondered for a moment, then spoke under his breath, "I think I just saw some kind of spirit."

Antonio was pointing and looking at the sky. "Did you see that American bald eagle, ladies?" he said.

Maria and Nanny were too busy chatting about Frankie's homerun and the Christmas day ahead of them to listen to Antonio.

"That eagle was amazing! And it seemed to just vanish," Antonio said.

Scratching his head confused, Antonio thought, I guess I didn't see it fly over a tree or something.

After they dropped Katie off at her home, Frankie and My Pig looked back at Katie's porch from the back of the truck. Katie and her parents were waving with big smiles as the truck continued down the dirt road. Frankie waved high in the air and My Pig oinked at Katie like he was saying thank you.

Frankie and his family arrived at home and got out of the truck.

"Wait here. Billy. I'll be right back with our fishing poles!" Frankie said.

Anna looked up at Antonio with a smile. "Oh, that was an amazing game, Papa," Anna said.

"It sure was, Anna," Antonio said.

Frankie came running from the porch, "Here you go, Billy, here's your pole."

"Th-thank you, which w-way is the p-pond?" Billy said.

"We just walk across the road and cut through the grape vines right over there," Frankie said.

"How c-cool, I've n-never f-fished before," Billy said.

"Don't worry, I'll show you how, Billy. Come on, My Pig. Let's show Billy the pond," Frankie said.

Maria and Nanny smiled warmly as they watched Frankie and his new friend Billy heading to the pond with My Pig trotting behind them.

Antonio and Anna stood on the porch watching Frankie disappear into the orchard. Their huge smiles were worth a thousand words.

All of a sudden a strong emotion took over Nanny. She stood looking into Maria's eyes and with a deep British accent she said, "Madam, may I say something to you?"

"Of course you can, Elaine."

It took a few seconds for her to get it out, and she did it with a hug. "Merry Christmas, Maria," Nanny said.

"Merry Christmas, Nanny," Maria said.

Anna looked amazed and turned to Antonio, "I can't believe it, Papa. Did you hear what Mama and Nanny just called each other? I think they just ended their debate."

Everyone's heads turned when they heard Frankie's voice

traveling through the orchard from the pond, "You got one, Billy! It's a bass!"

Antonio raised his hands to the sky and yelled, "Merrrry Christmas! Let the celebration begin!"

The End

CPSIA information can be obtained
at www.ICGtesting.com
Printed in the USA
FSOW02n1411120917
38647FS